WEST OF THE JORDAN

WEST
of the
JORDAN

A NOVEL

Laila Halaby

Beacon Press BOSTON

Beacon Press
25 Beacon Street
Boston, Massachusetts 02108-2892
www.beacon.org

Beacon Press books
are published under the auspices of
the Unitarian Universalist Association of Congregations.

07 06 05 04   8 7 6 5 4 3

Earlier versions of some of the chapters included here appeared in
The Hammer, Meridians, and *A Different Path: An Anthology of
the Radius of Arab American Writers.*

This book is printed on acid-free paper that meets the uncoated paper
ANSI/NISO specifications for permanence as revised in 1992.

Text design by Boskydell Design
Composition by Wilsted & Taylor Publishing Services

Library of Congress Cataloging-in-Publication Data

Halaby, Laila.
    West of the Jordan : a novel / Laila Halaby.
      p. cm.—(Bluestreak)
    ISBN 0-8070-8359-3 (alk. paper)
    1. Americans—Jordan—Fiction. 2. Arab American families—Fiction.
3. Female friendship—Fiction. 4. Jordan—Fiction. 5. Girls—Fiction.
I. Title. II. Series.
PS3608.A5455W47 2003
813'.6—dc21

                                                    2002154924

إلى أمل
وإلى دار أبو سعود سواعد

for Amal
and for the Abu Saud Sawaid family

MAKE IT DELICIOUS

You are late today.

Please do not be angry that I have taken so long, you write.

Don't rush.

Tell your news the way they tell their stories: slow and tasty . . . no rushing. Make it delicious like the olives, black and bursting with sweetness and sourness.

Remember the bottles of olive oil Um Saud gave you, and how you could drink a cup like a shot of whiskey, only without the burn, the white balls of cheese, sour with the bitterness of another land spread on bread so thick you could sleep under it.

Remember coming back from school, kicking dirt and passing dusty children up up up a road to the house where a meal and a family waited for you with loud kisses and steaming plates and many stories that you gobbled up or packed in your suitcases.

Stillness in dusty streets comes back when the sun shines, oceans and miles away.

That house told stories of courage and sadness and joy in every season, and now they come back to you at the wrong time, at the right time, at times that make you hate where you live, or love it more than you can make your words describe.

Cross the ocean, Abu Saud whispered, and take with you what you have learned, who you have seen, and the tastes that have nourished you, and please, do not forget us.

Now you sit in your sweet house with the desert outside and hostility all around you, thankful you have not forgotten altogether but wishing the memory could walk away a little further.

Please do not be angry I have taken so long, you write again, and soon a page is filled with news, congratulations for a baby's birth, and words of longing you cannot soften, you cannot hide.

As with every letter you have written since the dark night you left just over a dozen years ago, you write *Be careful and know that you are always with me. God keep you safe.*

You are late today, but try to remember the wisdoms you unpacked that lie scattered around your living room.

Don't rush . . . make it delicious.

L.H.
Tucson, 2003

PART ONE

HALA

1

....

GOING HOME

My gray, ankle-length dress scratches me everywhere, no matter how I shift in my regular-class, no-frills seat. It tickles my bottom and has a scooped back and scooped front, so people can peek from all angles. I thought the dress would give me confidence—mostly covering me, but pretty—but instead I fold myself, hunch, and calculate whether a tiny airplane bathroom is big enough to hold me as I change my clothes.

Next to me a diabetic Syrian woman has talked nonstop since our Royal Jordanian flight left LAX. Her body fills her seat and creeps into mine as well. Hennaed tendrils sneak from beneath her flowered scarf. She has lived in Los Angeles for thirty years and says that she does not speak a word of English.

"Why should I bother?" she shouts, so close to me that I taste her egg breath.

"You might enjoy it more," I suggest, trying not to inhale.

"Nothing to enjoy."

"Then why do you stay?"

"My children and grandchildren are there." She glares at me and clutches a cardboard box with pictures of hypodermic needles. "Can you please have a woman from the plane come here."

I pull my scratchy, gray shoulders up so they almost reach my neck, stretch my arm up, and push the button for the stewardess.

A slender, manicured finger pushes the button off and green eyes peer into mine. "Yes?"

The Syrian woman sits silently.

"She wanted me to ring for you," I say.

"What do you need, Auntie?" asks the stewardess, whose name tag reads "Nadia."

"I want you to know that I have to take these every day," she says, holding up the box of needles. "I don't know how to do it, so could you please get the plane's doctor to come and give me an injection." She smiles, exposing two gold teeth.

We stare at her. Nadia looks at me.

"We just met now," I say in English in case she thinks we are related.

"Let me see if I can find a doctor for you," she says.

The Syrian woman faces forward and says in a loud voice to no one in particular, "I have to go to the bathroom."

"Well, you should go then. They're very close." I point to the lavatories, just two rows away.

"I couldn't set foot in such a place!"

"Why not?"

"They're filled with the smell of dirty pigs."

"I beg your pardon?"

"You would use the same toilet, breathe the same air, as a strange man? I'd prefer exploding."

The Syrian woman stares at my scoops. I turn away.

It is early evening when the plane lands, the sun a dull orange on the runway. I stare out the window, brush my hair for the third time, and rub some of the shininess from my face.

I have come back to Jordan to visit my dying grandmother—my father's mother—one last time. I have been living with my mother's brother, Hamdi, and his American wife, Fay, in the United States for three years now.

"It's time for you to see your father," my uncle told me in the airport. "Stay with him for as long as you like and come back when you are ready. You are always welcome here."

My mother died two years ago. She sent me away because she knew she was dying, though I learned this later.

I am the youngest in a family that already had one boy, Jalal, and two girls, Latifa and Tihani. My mother was diagnosed with cancer just after my sister Tihani was born. It was caught early and my father sent her abroad for chemotherapy. The doctors said that she would make a full recovery. Tihani is six years older than I am, and in the time between our births, my mother miscarried four babies. Then she got pregnant with me. Between being physically drained from the miscarriages and her cancer and already being the mother of three children, she was a tired woman when I was born. She was never in good health and always suffered from one thing or another.

She adored me most—after Jalal—but she left much of the work in raising me to my oldest sister, Latifa, who was always a little slow. Latifa would take on all chores and tasks with great seriousness, admirable in an employee, unbearable in an older sister. If my mother had told her to throw me off the roof, she would have done so.

In dealing with me, she either tried to enforce my mother's rules exactly or tried to teach me how to do her chores. She had no sense of what I could and couldn't do at what age.

When I was four (she was twelve), she tried to teach me to iron. I burned my hand and one of my father's shirts and she yelled at me as though I had burned the house down. This incident started a cycle: Latifa would take care of me, then would do something so awful that my mother would take over. She would indulge me and cuddle me, and tell me stories and teach me embroidery and other things I can't imagine her ever having done with Latifa, who resented me more and more.

And then I would see my mother start to fade: fall asleep in the middle of her embroidery, curse when she dropped something, with words I had never heard anyone else use. (My mother had a distinct way of cursing herself when she was sick: "God damn your stupid, useless, jackass mother.") I tried to stay out of her way, but invariably Latifa would come to the rescue and take care of me, only this time a little angrier and more resentful than the time before. I learned that the only salvation from Latifa was avoidance, which is how it came to be that I spent a lot of time alone reading, a source of embarrassment or concern for almost everyone in my family.

"She will be blind before she is fifteen years old," Aunt Suha, my father's sister, would tell my mother every time she came over and found me bent over a book. "You shouldn't let her do this or no one will marry her."

My mother would nod, appeasing Aunt Suha enough to let the subject rest until the next time she came over. She never discouraged me, though, and liked to hear about the books I was reading, and read them herself if she had not done so previously. My father didn't approve of reading outside of school texts, and he used to take away my books when he came across them. Jalal was the only one beside my mother who encouraged me. He often countered my father's attempts by bringing me books he thought I'd find interesting, usually about animals or folktales from other countries.

During the summer before I was to start high school, Uncle Hamdi wrote from America to say that I could live with him and Fay, and that I could go to high school there. My mother was excited, perhaps because she thought I'd have a chance to finish what she barely started, or perhaps because she thought I'd have a freer education. Regardless, I was terrified at the thought of being away from my family, even though the idea of going to America—the America my mother had only tasted—*was* exciting. I was so tired of being made fun of for reading, for being too headstrong, for speaking my mind. My father said there was not a chance in the world that he would let such a young girl go live in America with only a maternal uncle and his American wife. He would not even listen to my mother's arguments and would leave the room when the discussion came up.

"Jalal has gone and come back and will stay to take care of the land. Tihani is married and away. Latifa is already old," my mother would call after him. "If Hala stays here she will rot like me and like Latifa. Look at us. We have rotted. Let Hala grow and dream."

At the time I didn't know why my father finally agreed to allow me to go—a year had passed since Uncle Hamdi's invitation, during which time I was enrolled at the American School in Amman—but he did and just as I started to grow and dream my mother died.

Even though my mother had lived in Jordan since she was nineteen, she was Palestinian and saw my father as something of a foreigner. In distance she was not so far from the home in which she grew up, but in reality, she was in another country—another household—with an entirely different way of thinking.

Her village, Nawara, is known for lovely, cleverly embroidered dresses (*rozas*) in an area of villages where almost no one embroiders, for lack of time and money. My mother was competent in embroidery, but she was not typical—even in her already nontypical village—and her interests lay elsewhere. Her father had a great deal of land in Ramallah, a city filled with ideas and energy. He knew about the world and he believed in education, which was why he let my mother go to America for college. Unfortunately, he also had a very traditional side to his thinking, which is how it came to be that my mother ended up marrying my father, an old foreigner, and why all three of her sisters married immediately after their graduation from high school.

The story goes that my father, a Jordanian landowner in his late thirties, saw my mother once when she was still in high school—he had been doing business with my grandfather for years and for the first time went home with him for a visit. He fell so in love with my mother that he offered my grandfather a large portion of his own land in Ramallah as dowry if she would marry him. At the time my grandfather refused, saying that she still needed to finish high school and was planning to go on to university, maybe abroad. After that, she alone would be free to accept or refuse the offer. My father announced that in spite of his age (more than twenty years her senior), he would wait until my mother gave him her answer. It turned out he had to wait less than a year, when my mother returned from the States in disgrace—thanks to the lies of her brother's friend. My father told my grandfather that regardless of the reason for my mother's return, his offer still held. My grandfather, sure that this was his last chance to find an acceptable match for his daughter, accepted the offer.

In the beginning of their marriage, my father was indulgent with my mother. He even offered to let her continue her studies, in Jordan. She refused—perhaps she was still heartsick—and began her role as wife and mother. Even though she was living this life she did not ask for, when Jalal was born she breathed her soul into him and spoiled him terribly. She was as happy as she could be, given the circumstances, and to this day Jalal is totally her child, the only one of those three who always makes sure that people know he is half Palestinian. Even in the late sixties and early seventies, when he risked being beaten, or worse, he would speak proudly of his mother and her country. (When Jalal married a few months ago, he insisted that it be to a girl from our mother's village, even though he has never lived in Nawara and has only visited a few times. At first my father refused, but Jalal insisted until my father agreed.)

For almost a year after Jalal's birth, my mother was happy. She didn't get pregnant again immediately, but my father wasn't in a rush since at least he had a son. Two years and a week after Jalal, Latifa was born. Almost two years after that, Tihani was born. That's when the difficulties in my family began. First, my mother got cancer. (The story I was told for years was that she was very sick and then she was well.) Then my father's recently widowed mother moved in with them. In 1967, the Occupation began and my father lost a lot of his land. My mother lost her freedom to visit her family. My father became less generous with my mother, and she became less generous with her children.

"It was bad for me. So much was expected, selflessly, and my thoughts were stuck on what might have been," she told me countless times. "I prayed so many times that if I could have one more healthy child, I would not try to have another one, and that I would be content with my life as it was. And then you were born, big and healthy and beautiful. You are my final blessing."

When she had the energy, she gave me everything. She

taught me the most complicated patterns in embroidery that she knew and told me equally complicated stories from her village as she was doing it. She took me wherever she went and explained everything to me. Best of all, she cuddled me endlessly, probably more than my brother and sisters combined. Latifa hated me for all these reasons: Latifa who drove my mother crazy; Latifa who had to deal with me every time my mother started to get sick; Latifa who hated me for the freedom I was allowed; Latifa who cared totally for my mother as she was dying.

If only I had known my mother was dying, then I would not have spent the last year of her life away. But perhaps if I never left, she would not have died in peace.

I see him before he sees me, and while I knew he would be alone, I wish he had brought Jalal, or even Latifa. As soon as he sees me coming down the escalator he sends a man to carry my bags.

My father looks old. His skin is dark, like fava beans, only more wrinkled, like raisins.

We embrace and he kisses me twice on both cheeks. "Thank God for your safe return, my daughter."

Odd to hear this kind voice after two years of silence. "And may God keep you safe," I reply.

Passing colorful people with their shouts and hugs and loud kisses and through the automatic doors, we walk into the evening that smells of diesel and toward a large black Mercedes parked under a sign that reads "No Parking."

"It's fatter than the last one," I say.

"I am?" he asks.

"No, the car."

"It's safer that way," he says and hands a folded bill to the wrinkled man who's put my bags in the trunk. We get in the car. "You look skinny," he says. "They don't feed you well, do they? Lazy goats."

I lean back in the soft leather. I can't erase the picture of my last visit, my mother's funeral, and then of the huge fight. The memory comes in my eyes, burning like the sun that's setting, but I keep my silence as we drive into the desert.

"How is your health?" I ask.

"Thank God for my good health. Even my doctor says he can't believe it." He lights a cigarette with the windows up and we drive in smoky silence.

We race the dust down the new highway on the way home to the outskirts of Amman.

"I loved your mother," he announces, perhaps seeing my memory. "God have mercy on her. Not a day passes that I don't think of her." He says this as though it's an apology.

I am silent. I do not want his stories or drunken, smoky lovesongs tossed in my lap. I want my mother back so much it aches. I want to hear her stories about her village, her words in my ears, her fingers stroking my hair.

MAWAL

2

....

NAWARA

*L*ots of places have special marks, while other places are just daytime normal with an occasional scary night, too thick silence, or a shrill scream to jazz them out of dusty boring.

You can tell about a place by the feeling you get from it, like creepy feeling places. That would be Um Lubna's house —it has spooky and nasty-curious airs about it, like you want to go look at what's going on inside, but that if you do a *jinn* might smack you, and if the *jinn* doesn't get you, then your mother will.

There's death feeling too, like too much sadness is falling out of a house and flooding the street, just to where you're standing, which is why you run away as fast as you can before it can touch you and creep up through your toes like the worms that make Egyptian workers sick.

People give those feelings too: one look at them and you get a feeling like sadness or greatness or beauty or misery or come-sit-with-me-so-I-can-tell-you-a-great-story. We have some of everybody in those categories, though more of I'm-ready-for-dinner, and have-you-already-fed-the-chickens? and don't-bother-me-I-have-work-to-do and don't-for-get-to-say-*bismallah-ar-rahman-ar-raheem*-before-you-squeeze-milk-from-the-goat's-teat people. It's those first ones who make the place a memory for other people.

Our village is called Nawara, which means flowers or blossoms. When you say it, *Naw-waar-a,* a hillside of small white wildflowers comes to mind, or the fragrant new blossoms on an orange or almond tree.

Everywhere is famous for something: political activism, delicious vegetables, ugly women. Our village is an island, famous for beautiful embroidered dresses that we call *rozas* while most everyone else calls them *thobes,* and yet surrounded by villages that do not embroider at all.

The complicated embroidery on our *rozas*—with both Palestinian and western stitches and patterns—captures the spirit of Nawara, which sits at the top of the West Bank, just west of the Jordan River, east of Jenin and far enough away from both of these places to be a peaceful village that only every so often releases an avalanche of stones and fire. This is something that happens more often as the Israelis take parts of our village to build their settlements.

Nawara could have a smaller version of herself in the United States, which is like an army calling all able-bodied young men away and then never returning the bodies.

You will find many women here grieving over sons and husbands who have forgotten them, or grieving over the evils that country has introduced their sons to, like drugs and drinking and loose women and gambling. My uncle Haydar lives in an American desert and stares at the sun because of the drugs he takes.

Um Radwan, our nosy next-door neighbor, is one of those women who is grieving over being forgotten. Her husband died when she was still young, with four sons and a daughter. The daughter works in Nablus and the sons all went to America. One of them married an American woman so the others could stay there. One died, one doesn't want to come back, and the other two come only every once in a while. They haven't forgotten her completely, though, and whenever someone else is coming home, they send suitcases full of presents, and I'm sure by now she has six or seven suitcases filled with comforters, sweaters, deodorant, soaps, aspirin, Kool-Aid, and laxatives. She's one of those people who covers her emptiness with harsh words, so no one will feel sorry for her. She does it on purpose, makes herself hard so no one can find her grieving. In our house, though, her guard goes down. Words like hair sneak out from beneath her proper head scarf and hint at grief that was pickled so long ago.

I know everyone's stories. I am my mother's only child and she had been married many years before she had me. All the waiting gave her patience and generosity. My father says that it also gave her ears that can hear even the worst story without her slapping back with unkind or judgmental words. She says she has room to be generous because she has been so blessed—a husband who did not divorce her even though she was childless for years, and a helpful daughter. Because I was always by my mother's side, people came to think of us as one, or as sisters, more than as mother and daughter, which is why women are not shy to pour out their troubles when I am in the room.

I think my mother has such listening power because what happened to her father was one of the worst stories the village knows. A big, powerful man with money and land and brains, killed by strangers, or by friends. No one ever found out. Slain on his own land, his young son, Uncle Haydar, a witness, but unable to identify the killers. Several years later two men who had had disputes with my grandfather were killed mysteriously. There were whispers that Haydar—the fastest runner Nawara has ever seen—had done it and then escaped to America on his brother's—Uncle Hamdi's—green card, but most people think the two killings were unrelated.

I think this background is what makes my mother pay attention to details and listen so well. So many women come spill their secrets and their joys and their agonies because they know my mother—and I—will keep them safe and do no more than stitch them into the fabric of our *rozas*.

I want to visit the States one day and see the life all of my cousins are leading that I hear about so much. That won't happen for a long time, maybe not until I am married, and I am not marrying one of those guys who left here when he was a teenager and has been living an American life ever since. I've seen their arrogance and I've heard stories.

That's all still some time away, though. I still have to finish high school, and then, if my parents will allow me, I want to go to college and become a teacher like Miss Maryam, who teaches English and Classical Arabic. She never married and is very giggly, so they call her a girl for both those reasons.

Life here follows the weather. In late fall and winter, the cold floors are like ice in the morning. The covers are as heavy as lead. Darkness sits and then the muezzin calls and then it's time, but there's nowhere to go to get warm. At school only the teachers and their favorites hover around the kerosene heater, and they scold you if you come close or even if you wear gloves in class. We have constant runny noses and the cold makes you play as hard as you can to stay warm. *Keep running so you never get cold.* Ours is a cold house with one room like a sauna; the portable heater is going, and everyone is quiet, exhausted from the cold, then the heat. Food smells of itself and you cannot escape.

When the rain comes, it turns everything to mud and makes the cold worse because it's wet and never dries. Our windows fog, food smells damp, and light turns an ugly yellow, making it impossible to sew or read. Water is everywhere and mud is everywhere else.

Television in our house is like a loud monkey: it never shuts up when it's awake, and it always holds everyone's attention no matter how silly its behavior. Sometimes I watch it while I study, especially the music videos, but my mother tells me to stop because I often get distracted and get up to dance with the song.

Almost everyone has a television, even if they only own two dresses and one bag of rice, a television and a VCR to watch weddings over and over and over. Girls like to watch themselves and see how pretty they looked; men like to see that too if the women let them. Almost everyone has relatives in the States or in the Gulf and it lets us have a chance to watch those faraway sons, cousins, brothers, sisters, neighbors.

My father has one sister and two brothers, and they live in Nawara. But all of my mother's brothers and sisters have gone away, all to America except for Auntie Huda. She had four children and lived in Jordan. She died two years ago of cancer, and the saddest thing was that Hala, her youngest daughter, was studying in America and didn't know how sick her mother was, so she didn't come home and didn't see her mother before she died.

My other two aunties, Shahira and Maysoun, went to the States with their husbands. Shahira has six kids and Maysoun has three. Uncle Hamdi and Uncle Haydar are in the States too, but they don't have children, unless you count that Hala lives with Hamdi now. I have so many cousins. I have met most of them, though not Shahira's youngest four, Khadija and her three brothers. Their father is poor so they cannot visit. Khadija looks so sweet and she always makes me laugh because she has such an Arab face and such an American accent. I love to watch the new fashions and accents of my American cousins in the videotapes they send.

Spring is clean and the sun rises victorious, returns smiles to people's faces, returns energy to their bones. Clean air carries the scent of jasmine or orange blossom or diesel. Loud voices and great silence, so you can devour the sky or float in your dreams. An odd stirring creeps inside me which I can't explain, though most of my friends show hints of a similar restless quality.

And now, as summer begins, I want to lie on my back and eat the sky. I want to be mischievous. I want to stare at Miss Maryam's large pointed breasts, to stand this much closer to the vegetable man who winks, to let him touch my hand when he gives me back my change.

My mother has led me to believe that feelings and thoughts such as these will take me straight to hell, or make me turn out like my untame cousin Soraya, *who ate too much cereal when she was young and has the foolishness of an American in her blood,* and that may be true but I don't much care. I want to sit in the garden and hike my dress up to my knees so my legs can feel the sun as it kisses them.

Big-mouth village. This one farts during morning prayers and by midmorning they're talking in the coffee shops that I'm not allowed to enter about the three bowls of *fool* he ate that morning and how there has never been a louder fart.

Worst big-mouth thing I know is what happened to late Auntie Huda when she was young. Smart girl, like clean, spring morning air. Good girl too, like never been hit for something she did, never thought something bad, always straight with everyone she talked to. Sweet and gentle, pretty, not beautiful, which is how everyone describes Hala, who I've only met a few times.

My uncle Hamdi was in Arizona, in big, greedy America. Huda applied and got accepted by the university there, the same one Hamdi was attending and would later teach at. My grandmother, who is Bedouin, was—and is—conservative like a girdle, but my grandfather had land in Ramallah and was different from anyone else. He was open to new ideas. Against the advice of the entire village, he let her go to America and live with her brother while she studied.

"There is nothing wrong with letting a girl learn as much as a boy does. That is our only hope," he repeated to the many doubters.

Because it still took her a long time to read and write in English, school was harder in the States and she had to study very late at the library sometimes. My uncle didn't care; he was always up studying too.

Huda became friends and maybe fell in love with a boy from Jerusalem. Their relationship was formal, Arab-style. He walked her to class, to the library, had lunch with her in the university cafeteria. He lived close to the university with his sister and her husband and sometimes Huda would go to study there when the library closed.

One night it was pouring rain and Huda and the boy were at the library. His car wouldn't start and his sister and her husband were out of town with their car. She called Hamdi to pick her up, but he lived in another part of the city and said that the storm was really bad and *just stay where you are because it's not safe to drive in this weather* and *I'll pick you up when it stops, or in the morning, whichever comes first.* So they ran to his house in the pouring, pouring rain. That night she stayed at his house and slept in the sister's room.

It just so happened that there was a boy from our village who was at Hamdi's house that evening. He also happened to be a big liar, and talked to his gossipy mother the next day on the phone and he told her something like: *I am fine and I see Hamdi Salaama a fair amount, and his sister, of course. Yes, she's studying. Well, she's really not so good. If you'll keep this to yourself, I'll tell you. Promise, Yama? Well, she's not so proper and last night she didn't come home at all. Why indeed? She was spending the night at her boyfriend's house.*

Within hours the entire village knew what had happened. My grandmother was hysterical, tearing her clothes and weeping as if Huda had died. My grandfather was more up-set because he was furious too. He ordered his son to send her home or she would not have a home to return to. Huda got back from the library that next evening and found Hamdi sitting quietly. He handed her a plane ticket, which she had to use in the next two days, or be disowned by her parents, *even though I told them it was a lie and I swore on the Quran and on the lives of our mother and her mother before her.*

She came back, and eventually the whole thing straight-ened itself out and her parents came to know that she was telling the truth, and the liar boy denied he had ever said any-thing, but by then it was too late and Huda was back here. It was no surprise that shortly after her return she was married to an older Jordanian man and left Nawara forever. Some-where inside me I wished so badly that the boy from Jeru-salem had followed her back from America and asked her to marry him. What a disappointment when she practically proved her guilt by marrying an old man and leaving her country to live with him.

Big-mouth village. Sad love-story girl.

But mostly everyone else is like rice without enough salt, who you only remember because you see them everyday, and not like the hot pepper ones, who you remember because of the burn they leave.

Summers and weddings are the best things, especially the weddings that are built on foreign money. For all the difficulties we are having, people still like to show off how much money they have. When my cousin Jalal, Huda's eldest son, came from Jordan to marry Jawahir Sulayman, they had a traditional wedding that lasted three days—he even carried her off on a horse—and my mother complained that the cost of the wedding would have paved a street, built a mosque—though we certainly don't need another one—even created a school, and that it was shameful to spend it all on a wedding.

I don't agree with her. Almost everyone goes to weddings and has a good time because they forget their problems, even my mother, who complained before and afterward, but managed to spend those three days dancing and laughing and cooking and chanting. All the old ladies dance and remember their youth, while the men sit around and feel good about their lives, even if they don't at non-wedding times. Everyone dances and the kids eat sweets for days.

Weddings, especially the big ones, are for showing off: your gold, your clothes, your daughters. (The saddest is to see an older lady without much gold and know that she has been through financial hardship and had to sell it all.) Women like to wear their fanciest dresses—either traditional *rozas* soaked with clever embroidery or modern dresses of shiny black material with gold spray or satiny pink that wrinkles and makes them sweat, dancing in those closed rooms and everyone smelling like themselves. There is so much excitement. Even the old old women get up strength they do not seem to possess at any other time, and they dance and chant and sing and give their sharpest ululations for the bride.

I love to watch the dancing. Women show happiness and calm that they keep buried during other days. The best dancer from our village is my American cousin Soraya. My mother cannot say her name without pleading to God to help her soul, and praying that I never become the way she is. But even she agrees that instead of having magic fingers that can stitch the finest pattern on material, she has the magic directly in her hips and legs.

And everyday there is enough talk to fill the skies: about So-and-So who sold his land to the Israelis, *may God curse him,* about the checkpoints and the endless humiliation, but also about this person's marriage and that person's graduation and that one who had the most beautiful baby ever seen, and even that other one who has been gone so long that no one remembers what he looks like, yet he still sends money to the wife he divorced a generation ago.

Sometimes the skies that wander over Nawara are blue, other times they are gray and gloomy. They paint our days different colors, and sometimes they watch over our blossoming village like a child about to bury his nose in the whitest flower on the hillside.

SORAYA

3

....

FIRE

I have fire.

Everyone knows it. They see it in my beautiful brown exotic eyes that I paint full of Maybelline kohl to turn my tears black.

"She's Arabian," they say at my high school as I pass by them. "In her country they don't have furniture or dishwashers, only oil."

I tell them what they want to hear, which is nasty stories about young men sticking their things into goats and some twelve-year-old girl being carried off on a camel to be third wife to old Shaykh So-and-So and the five oil wells my father owns.

My mother exploded the first time she heard about a story I told. "You have to show the best of us, not the ugly lies."

But I let my ambassador sister and cousins do that while I talk ghetto slang.

"That's not English!" my sister yells.

"My ass this ain't English!" I yell back.

My mother is disappointed that I am not a good daughter, but she won't admit that she has anything to do with it and says instead that I have a weak spirit and have been "taken in by the lie that is America: freedom, freedom, freedom." I know she can't wait until next year is over and I'm done with high school so she can marry me off and concentrate on the things that matter to her, like her house and her hair.

My sister and cousins are the way my mother wishes I were and she is always comparing us and telling me what good girls they are and how I am just a headache. "You are like labor that never ends: pain everywhere all the time." She can't accept that my way of being different is just as good as everyone else's way of being the same. I like to enjoy myself, unlike my sister Pauline who, despite her American name, is very conservative and believes that all answers lie in God's words and that suffering is good. My cousin Khadija is conservative too, but I like her, except when her parents are around and she acts stupid like she can't think for herself.

Mawal, who lives in Nawara, would be my mother's version of perfect if she weren't so fat, like her mother, Aunt Saher. They are twins, famous for sitting still and eating up people's stories, gobbling them like *maqluba*. Everyone from our family and from our village goes to them. They bring their problems or aches or secrets with them. Like helium in super-stretch balloons that get bigger and bigger and never explode, my aunt and cousin accommodate any hardship. Then the people leave, their burdens gone, and my aunt and cousin are a little fatter than before.

My cousin Hala, who didn't grow up here and lives in Arizona now, is my mother's favorite because she is "such a good Arab girl," but I say she is boring with a capital *B* and even my mother agrees that she should get her nose out of books more often. Hala has Auntie Fay wrapped around her finger and willing to give her all the freedom in the world, and all she wants to do is sit at home and read.

My mother is the strong one in our house and people

would probably make fun of my father if it weren't for all the money he has. Money is his favorite thing, like somewhere along the way he decided he could only focus on one thing and he thought better money than family, less headaches. So men respect him because of his success. He owns a grocery store in Hollywood, but he got his money from other business ventures.

People are always coming to our house to visit, which is my mother's favorite activity and why our house is always spotless, why she has so many clothes, and why there is always so much food. A few weeks ago my cousin Lina (my father's niece) came over with Jaffer, her fiancé, and her mother, Auntie Dahlia. They were talking about their upcoming wedding. I love going to weddings, but my mother hates me to go and worries that I will do something she thinks is unacceptable, like what happened when we were in Nawara and went to my cousin Jalal's wedding. The story comes up all the time, so it wasn't surprising when my mother told Lina and Jaffer that it was too bad they weren't going home to have a traditional wedding like cousin Jalal, that Lina remembered that she hadn't seen the video and that she had been meaning to ask my mother to borrow it. My mother tried to talk them out of it but with no success, and somehow got them so excited that they wanted to watch it then and there.

> *Your eyes are the light of my eyes.*
> *For you I sing this song.*

It starts out modern flowery style. "Show-off video" is what we call it when tapes have fancy editing like this. I knew my mother was hoping that Lina and Jaffer would get bored before we got to the *henna*, which was the second day of the wedding, but they didn't and so we watched it. This part shows just the women, the older ones and the married ones in colorful traditional dresses, the younger ones in longer western dresses, and the bride in a sequined blue gown, sitting in a chair way up high on top of a table at one end of the room. The women have already painted her hands with *henna* designs and now they call for her to dance. At first she refuses and lowers her eyes shyly. "Such a good girl," my mother always says at this point.

> *Your eyes are the light of my eyes.*
> *For you I sing this song.*

I know they are watching Jalal's new wife get up off her pedestal, helped up and then down by little-girl hands begging for the bride to dance her dance. I know their expressions will change when the bride has finished dancing alone and the other women join in.

I glance at Jaffer, who watches all of the girls in this video with too much interest. Lina sits next to him wearing her ever-present polite smile. I know they are watching me dance with the bride, my back to the camera.

"Wow, she knows how to shake it," Jaffer says.

My mother's eyes dart in my direction.

"She's really shaking it," he shouts.

Jaffer's mother points. "She's good."

"Mmm," says Lina.

"Who is that girl who's shaking her dance all over the place?" Jaffer asks with glassy eyes, looking like those boys at school who stare at the posters of naked ladies in their lockers.

My mother and I look at each other. I know she is mixed between angry and furious. She always wants to do what's just right and appropriate and doesn't want anyone talking bad about her.

I leave the room to prepare more tea, cookies, fruits, anything that will get me out of the room while I hear my ashamed mother explaining that the girl dancing, *ilee bithiz,* who is "shaking it," is me, her daughter, his soon-to-be cousin, and would he please calm himself down. Hasn't he been paying attention? I have been wearing the same—"too tight"—dress throughout this portion of the video. How could you not have realized?

> *Your eyes are the light of my eyes.*
> *For you I sing this song.*

Once I danced every night in a black slip with a candle burning in front of a barred window that often had Israeli soldiers on the other side of it.

It was only a room in my grandmother's house in boring little Nawara, but *hiz hiz hiz* the way my feet taught my hips to follow the drumbeats, I imagined I was an imprisoned princess and the man who watched me from behind his gun was my evil captor. I would dance every night, waiting for the heroic prince who would rescue me and love me until the drumbeats stopped, which would be never.

I don't tell my cousin's fiancé this, of course, and he lowers his eyes when I serve them tea.

> *Your eyes are the light of my eyes.*
> *For you I sing this song.*

This year I told my family a thousand and one lies and went to a disco and danced for a beautiful man who came to love me, love me so much that I carried his credit card, wore his jewelry, and had lunch with him until I satisfied him in every way. Then he returned to his blond American wife and two blond American children while I folded myself into the boxes that once bulged with sparkling promises, waiting for the ache to leave, which it did eventually. Dance, shake it all out—*hiz hiz hiz*—with eyes closed and hips racing those awful drums.

Jaffer is back to normal, once again the man who wouldn't shake my hand when he arrived at our house because he had already washed for prayer. The glassy look has dribbled into gossipy interest, and Lina is absorbed by the dresses and waistlines of our faraway relatives.

It always happens like this: when it comes time for the women to dance, I put them to shame. Even when I was little it happened like that. I don't know where it comes from, but they know it too—it's fire. They talk about how bad I am, especially at weddings in the States, because I dance shamelessly where men can see me and not just in front of other women and a camera.

"But if we are all supposed to dance and this is one of the places where mothers see a girl they like and go tell their sons about them, then why is it bad if I dance better than the rest of you?"

"It is not proper to behave like that, like a loose woman," my mother says.

"But if I'm happy, what's wrong with that?"

"You shouldn't show it. Finish." My mother doesn't like to argue, which is probably why she didn't object when I told her I wanted to bring Ginna Simms to Lina's wedding.

Ginna Simms lives next door to us here in Glendale and is the weirdest mix of Russian and Black and Chinese and Puerto Rican. She is a few years older than me and lives with her old mother and two young sons. She tells everyone that her husband was killed in a car accident, but I know the truth is that he's a drug addict and not her husband. I also know she goes with a lot of men and watches nasty videos. I know about the videos because I watch them with her sometimes. The first time I saw one, her mother was asleep in her room and the moans and groans were so loud I was sure that it would wake her up.

"She's deaf, don't worry," Ginna said, smiling a smile that made me uncomfortable. "You don't like it?" she kept asking.

"It's okay," I told her.

Then I saw another one and another and I got used to them. Now I don't mind watching them—some of them, that is. Sometimes Ginna brings ones where there are a lot of people together and close-ups of everything and they are nasty with a capital *N*. I refuse to watch them, but I like some new ones that are fairy-tale style, where the woman is so pretty and the man is kind of handsome and she is irresistible for him.

My body is like some of those women. I have a skinny girl's waist with woman hips and large breasts. I know my body is sexy; I can tell by the way men look at me, by the way men have always looked at me. I try to hide it in front of my family, and most days I go to school early so I can change out of my loose pants and elbow-length shirts into tighter clothes that make my body show more. Some of the girls are jealous of me because I am like a woman and they are still little girls, but more because guys like me even though I'm not easy like some girls, but if I like someone, then I'll make him happy. Not to mention that I am exotic.

I like to have fun, to enjoy myself and to feel good. I have always been that way. My mother tells me how wrong this is, like it is evil or something and my sister says the same thing. I think they think it's wrong because they don't know what it is to be satisfied, and it scares them. It seems all of the women in our family are like this. Even though married ladies talk about sex, it is always within the context of a marriage and you have to have been a virgin. At least my parents aren't as bad as Khadija's father, who thinks that his daughter's reputation is the most important thing in the world.

Her father hits her and her brothers for anything. One time Khadija took two dollars from her older brother, Muhammad, to buy a barrette. Her mother wouldn't pay for it because they have no extra money ever and she doesn't think she should spoil her, so she took it from Muhammad who got really mad when he realized that she was the one who took it. That day when he came home from school, he told his father that he saw Khadija at school kissing a boy behind the gym during lunch hour. Khadija's father didn't ask her if it was true, he just came after her with a belt, yelling *slut* and *whore* at her. She didn't go to school for two days, and the next time I saw her she wouldn't look at me, just held her head down like her shoes were the prettiest things ever.

When it came time for Lina's wedding, I invited Ginna so I'd have a friend there instead of just my critical relatives and my boring cousins. I even taught her to dance Arabic style, which was very easy for her, probably because she has so many different kinds of blood in her that they all move in different ways. (You should see her dance those sexy Latin kinds of dances. The guys all think she's hotter than hot, flyer than fly.) Ginna knows how conservative our culture is, though, so she didn't wear one of her usual tight little skirts, just a dress that reached her ankles that made my mother tell her how nice she looked and how glad she was that she was joining us and that she hoped she'd enjoy herself.

My parents are from the same village in the West Bank, and half of the village lives here in Glendale or Hollywood or Anaheim. The older people all act the same way they did when they were home, which isn't fair in a lot of ways because we're in America now, but they tell us that we are not supposed to be living an American life.

When we got to the hotel, we saw some of the old village ladies coming up from the parking lot dressed in their best show-off *rozas*. They looked so out of place—those short lit-tle thick-waisted women with flowing white scarves and all their youth's gold dripping off them, almost from another planet.

Ginna smiled. "Look how pretty they look."

We went into the ballroom that had been reserved for the reception. Lina looked so pretty in her fancy white dress, sitting with her new husband, Jaffer, at a table at the front of the room. Jaffer's family has been very successful in this coun-try so the wedding had lots of decorations, there was a good band playing, and Lina was heavy with gold. Theirs was a love marriage, at least in that they chose each other, so she showed her happiness more than a lot of brides do.

We went to our table and sat down. Two old ladies came and greeted us and I introduced Ginna, who smiled sweetly and said, "*Marhaba*."

"They wear so much gold," she whispered, her eyes stuck on the golden coin headband of one of the women.

"Weddings are for showing off," I told her when they walked away.

"Tsst," hissed my mother, who was wearing her newest *roza* with gold threads and all the jewelry she owns.

We watched the people coming through the door and Ginna seemed to be enjoying it. I saw her looking at the young guys who were coming in. "If they're here this early, they're either too young, religious, or married," I whispered in her ear.

"Can you believe Esmerelda is wearing that dress? It's much too tight," said my mother before Esmerelda came over and kissed her on both cheeks. On and on like this, and then eating then singing then dancing, first the older women then the younger ones.

Khadija came up to us and kissed my mother and then me

on both cheeks. She had her hair pulled back in a thick braid and wore a ruffly pink dress that made her look like an overgrown doll. I introduced her to Ginna, who smiled and said, "*Marhaba*. You look very pretty, Khadija."

"Thank you. So do you." Khadija looked embarrassed, and though she stared at her feet I could tell she was flattered.

"Are you going to dance?" asked Ginna.

"She hates to dance," I said, trying to spare Khadija having to explain.

"Why don't we all dance together?" Ginna said. At first Khadija looked down and didn't say anything, but then, to my surprise, she nodded. Ginna and I got up and we both held Khadija's hands as we walked toward the front of the room to where the women were dancing. I could feel the eyes on me as we joined in their circle, but I danced like the rest of them, nothing flashy, no show-off shaking. Ginna danced conservatively too, as though she were also from our village and had been doing this forever. I had told Ginna about Khadija before and she had felt sorry for her, which is probably why she was so nice to her now, watching her the whole time and telling her what a good dancer she was. It was nice to see Khadija smiling and her eyes laughing.

As we danced, I looked to see who was in the band and Fadi winked at me. He graduated from my school last year and we used to hang out together, but in front of my family I pretend I don't know him more than to say a formal hello. I looked at Lina, who was trying to tell me something with gestures, which is why I didn't notice when Khadija's father stepped into our group and grabbed Khadija.

"Slut," he said to Ginna, loud enough that the other women could hear him, but not loud enough that the people who were not dancing could hear. "How dare you lay a hand on my daughter."

Ginna had stopped dancing and was staring at him. "Fuck you," she said.

"Uncle . . ." I started to say.

"Don't you dare talk to me," he said, turning toward me. "Don't dirty your family with this person." He spat and looked back at Ginna. "Don't you ever get near my daughter again."

Khadija looked as though she would crumble with humiliation as her father dragged her off. I felt a knife go through me.

Some of the women who had heard his words continued dancing, pretending nothing had happened, but others stopped. Esmerelda cursed Khadija's father in Arabic and said he was an old shoe with a hole in his head as well as one in his ass.

"Don't pay any attention to him," Esmerelda told Ginna. "He is crazy."

"Ignore him," cried Um Ghazi from the other side of the circle. "He treats his children worse than stray dogs, how can you take seriously the words of a man like that?"

Still, Ginna was furious. "What an asshole. How can he talk like that and no one says anything?"

Her curse words sounded very loud and naked and bad in front of those old ladies. "He is like that," I told her. "Everyone is used to his outbursts. There's nothing you can do, and it's better to stay out of his way."

"How can he be so horrible to that little girl?" she said, still talking loudly as we walked back to our table. "Soraya, I don't want to be rude or to insult you, but I would like to leave. I am not comfortable here."

Suddenly the humiliation that Khadija had on her face drenched me. I felt dirty, as if I was walking naked and people were throwing mud at me.

"Why did you stop dancing so soon?" my mother asked when we got to our table. "And what happened to Khadija? I saw her father dragging her off like a criminal."

"He's an asshole," I told her.

"*Haram alayki,*" she spat. I knew she was thinking that I did something wrong again.

"Ginna and I are going home."

"You don't have to go," Ginna said to me, and then turned to my mother. "I'm not feeling well, but you should stay and enjoy yourselves. I'll get a cab."

"Scandalous daughter," my mother said to me in Arabic as Ginna picked up her purse and jacket. "You even manage to offend your own friends." She got up and walked to another table.

I wanted to shout something at her, but I didn't have the energy, so I said good-bye to Ginna and sat down in my mother's seat, feeling as though someone had poured acid into my belly. All those ladies heard my uncle's stupid words, but no one stopped him, like a wild dog allowed to bite everyone. The worst burn was Ginna and all those things she must be thinking about me.

I sat at the table for the rest of the evening, numb and burning first with anger then with an awful kind of dirty embarrassment. I hated my uncle more in that moment than I have ever hated anyone. I couldn't think up words ugly enough to describe him. I hated my mother for blaming me and I hated Ginna for not staying.

"Can you believe how young Esmerelda looks?" my mother asked me later when she came and sat next to me again, forgetting that she was mad at me. I nodded, still burning too much to say anything.

4

....

SAND AND FIRE

*K*hadija. In Islam, Khadija was the Prophet Muhammad's wife. She was much older than he was and had a lot of money. He was said to have loved her very much.

In America my name sounds like someone throwing up or falling off a bicycle. If they can get the first part of it right, the "Kha" part, it comes out like clearing your throat after eating ice cream. Usually they say *Kadeeja,* though, which sounds clattering clumsy. It never comes out my mother's soft way; *she* makes it sound almost pretty.

It's not like I'm dying to have an American name. I'd just like a different Arabic one. There are so many pretty names: Amani, Hala, Rawda, Mawal, and they all mean such pretty things—wishes, halo, garden, melody—not just the name of a rich old woman. My father would slap me if he heard me say that. I'm sure the original Khadija was very nice and that's why the Prophet Muhammad married her and why my father gave me her name, but I'm also sure that if the original Khadija went to school in America that she would hate her name just as much as I do.

I think Princess Diana is beautiful, and even though Diana is a pretty western name, I thought I'd like to have it, so I told my friends at school that I was going to change my name to Diana and they should call me that from now on.

"But you don't look like a Diana," Roberta told me.

"What do I look like then?"

"I don't know. Like a Kadeeja, I guess."

My father is a mechanic. He is very clever with fixing things and our little house is always filled with tools and engine parts. He works as a third mechanic in a nearby repair shop. The "third" means that he is the extra, *yaani*, if they have a lot of business, then he has a good job. "Which is not often enough," my mother says to explain the foreign-looking shame money we get sent every month to buy our groceries with.

My father has many dreams that have been filled with sand. That's what he tells me: "This country has taken my dreams that used to float like those giant balloons, and filled them with sand. Now they don't float, and you can't even see what they are anymore."

I try to be understanding, but I wish my father wouldn't tell me these things. I feel empty and scary and have that stomach feeling like something awful will happen.

My mother seems too busy to have lost any dreams, and she never talks to me about things like that, only about house things and taking-care-of-your-brothers things, and sometimes don't-do-that-or-you'll-never-marry things.

Sometimes my father loves my mother—and the rest of us—so much that he becomes a kissing and hugging machine. Sometimes, though, he is an angry machine that sees suspicious moves in every breath. But most of the time he is sad, his thoughts somewhere I cannot visit.

I'll tell you what the scariest thing is: when he drinks. He doesn't do it that often and he doesn't have to drink that much before his eyes become bullets, his fists the curled hands of a boxer, and our living room the ring of *Monday Night Wrestling*.

"It's fire from hell," my mother says about the liquor.

I believe it. One time I went into the yard to look for a ball I had lost in the bushes the day before, and I found my father drinking. He grabbed my arm and held his bottle in front of me. "Drink," he said.

I didn't say anything.

"Drink, girl. What's wrong with you?"

"You said we should never drink from that."

"Well, you should always do as I say, and I want you to try it this time so you know what not to drink."

It sort of made sense, but I had a feeling I should not do it.

"Drink," he insisted and stuck the bottle under my nose. It had a horrible smell and I turned my face away.

"Drink, girl, and you'll never have to drink again."

I took the bottle, held my nose, and put it to my lips. As I lifted it in the air I felt fire catch on my lips and in my mouth and I spat it back out. My father glared at me. I got the stomach feeling.

"Drink."

I lifted the bottle again and I felt the burn on my tongue, on my throat, and down the inside of my neck. I swallowed fire. My father just sat and stared. He took the bottle from me, closed the top, put it back in the box, locked it, and stood up. I remained where I was, but the fire went from my belly to his eyes and he pulled me by the arm and then by the ear and dragged me into the kitchen where my mother was cutting vegetables.

"Oh Mother of Shit," he called to her. "Your little dog of a daughter has been drinking. Smell her mouth."

My mother leaned over and sniffed my mouth and I closed my eyes. She slapped my face and the fire came back to me.

"He made me drink it," I screamed, and saw my father's eyes enlarge.

"A drinker and a liar!" he shouted, and started hitting me everywhere. I screamed and screamed and finally got free and ran to my room. I opened the closet and closed the door behind me and prayed to God the fire would burn somewhere else.

"My ache comes from losing my home," my father tells us a lot. Part of me understands that, because I see him unhappy and feeling different than everyone else here, but part of me doesn't understand. I see my uncles and cousins and neighbors, and they seem to be doing just fine. So mostly I try to stay out of his way.

My mother's mother, who lives in Nawara, is dying. Ma wants to go home and stay with her, but Baba says there is no money. This makes Ma quiet, sometimes for a day or two. "I am trapped," she yells at him.

Finally, I feel sorry for her too.

PART TWO

5

....

MOURNING

I bring the coffee. I mixed in extra cardamom because ours is a house of mourning and I think it will calm the spirits. The smell soothes me as the steam from the cups curls into my nose. I carry the tray with eight saucers stacked up and eight demitasses side by side filled with coffee.

The house is quiet even though it is an early summer morning. There are many people in our living room, but they are silent now. I am careful not to let my slippers drag too much on the floor when I walk.

Thin pale hands with coral chips at the end of each finger reach out to pick up a cup and saucer. Even in mourning Aunt Suha is lovely, perhaps more so than usual.

I move around the circle serving coffee to lowered eyes until my tray is empty and I return to a chair in the corner next to Latifa.

There is a shadow at the door. Uncle Abbas, Aunt Suha's husband, enters the room bowing his head. "May God give safety to the heads of everyone in this house."

"God protect you," we answer.

"God keep you safe and preserve your children," says Latifa, who always has to have the last word, regardless of the occasion.

Aunt Suha begins to wail for the spirit of my grandmother, her mother. The other women follow.

I watch them.

My brother Jalal serves the welcoming coffee, which is bitter. Uncle Abbas drinks from the cup once and shakes it so that Jalal will take it and return it and the pot to the table by the door.

"We are to God and to him we return," says Uncle Abbas, and the women begin to wail again.

This visiting will last three days. Our house will contain death for forty more as the older women dress in black to remember those departed.

Two years ago, there were many more figures in black and more wailing. It was my mother's death then that was being mourned, and, like today, people spoke of God and it being her time.

I was in my English class at my high school in Tucson and was called down to the principal's office. It was spring and it smelled of orange blossoms. When I saw Uncle Hamdi waiting there, I knew before he spoke that my mother was dead, though it was not until much later that I learned it was a death predicted, a death that was slow and painful in coming. Later, I pieced it all together and could understand Aunt Fay's hugging me some mornings and my mother's long phone calls that had seemed so extravagant. No one told me how serious her condition was. Toward the end, I didn't know that it was days, not years, she was seeing ahead of her, and so I did not go home, did not say good-bye properly.

Hamdi and Fay and I flew home to Jordan. That's when I

learned that this last bout with cancer had been diagnosed as fatal shortly before I came to America. My mother knew that she would die, and the only request she made of my father was that I be allowed to go to America.

While she was alive, my father respected her wishes, but not even two days into my mourning her death, he made it clear that he was going to be the one to make the decisions about my life from then on.

"Hala, it is time for you to be with your family, for you to finish your studies here," he told me. I didn't respond. I could not think of anything beyond my emptiness and aching. For days all I did was lie in bed and cry and think about my mother.

Just before Hamdi and Fay were to go back, my father came to me again. "Hala, it is time for you to be with your family. I'm sure you understand. You must think about your life now, and plan to put your roots here as a woman."

A screen lifted from my eyes. I was to replace my mother with a husband. I was to stay in Jordan forever. Marry—engaged even before high school was over. Have children. Be someone else's burden.

Maybe I spoke because I had learned how to move my tongue like an American. Maybe it was just my grief that made me lose control. Or anger.

"I am going back with Hamdi and Fay."

"You will stay here. You have no more need for them."

Strength came holding the hand of rage. "My mother's wish was that I study in America. If I stay here, I will kill myself. I will go to my mother and then you will have the blood of two people on your hands."

He stared at me. No yelling. No cursing. No invitations to kill myself this very minute at his feet—something I surely would never have been able to do even with my grief at its strongest. Just staring. He turned and walked away. We did not speak again. Jalal took us to the airport and my father did not come to say good-bye. In one week, I lost both my parents.

Fay held my hand for most of the flight back. "We are your family and we love you," she kept saying. "He will come around, you'll see. Give him time."

Stitch with red for blood.

Stitch with white for purity.

Pull it all out and sit in black for death.

6

....

CROSSING

As my mother puts it, Huda was the first lovely Nawarese girl dragged by marriage across the river Jordan, but not the last.

"As life gets harder, more fathers are willing to release their daughters to a different world."

And then their mothers come and weep and lick their wounds in my mother's house—like Farah, a neighbor who is married to my mother's uncle Bajis. She is a serious woman and is not friendly with many people, but together, she and my mother are like sisters.

Her voice is thick as she spills her sadness. . . .

Spring is the beginning of life. Spring is the end of life.

"Go back. Go back," the daughter told her mother's stone face. "Your other children are waiting for you and I will come visit you soon, God willing."

Mother and daughter said good-bye before they reached the bridge that crosses the river Jordan. The mother's heart broke, but her face stayed smooth, her sadness showing only in the darkness of her blood, in the eggplant color her face became as she folded the sadness into herself, ate it like an almond nowhere near ripe.

It used to be that those were the joys: almonds in spring, figs in summer, olives in fall, memories in winter, mulberries in spring. But now everything was bleak winter memories, even the fruits hanging heavy on the trees, all bursting with what was and what will never be again.

We are from God and to Him we return.

Born crying-screaming, dying crying-whispering: a baby with no words to express his pain, only shrieks; an old woman with all the words in the world clattering inside her and she keeps her mouth clamped shut for fear the loudness will escape.

But I am not an old woman, said Farah to herself. I am barely forty. I could live to be twice this age. The thought made her heavy as she waited, waited with all the other women who were crossing the bridge, going home, envying the foreigners who could cross from another spot with nothing more than a stamped paper for their passports.

Farah said nothing, did not try to make conversation with anyone and resented those women who did. This was not the time for chatting, she thought to herself. For the sake of your dignity, please stop. She tried to make her thoughts envelop the three women in front of her, talking as though they were at a wedding. She tucked her pain deep inside so that no strip search, no matter how thorough, would ever find it.

As the long bundle of women moved, the body smells got heavier, and though Farah felt her head swoon with nausea, she did not flinch, showed no sign of her thoughts as she waited, waited, watching. Old women and young girls, and young girls with babies, and *slap,* it came back to her where she had just been and the awfulness of it and how there was no way to change it, just accept God's will and teach yourself rigidity. Teach yourself to keep all of the pain in one small corner inside. Farah kept hers behind her right breast, thinking the kindness from her heart might sneak over and color the black and gray some gorgeous orange color.

They moved slowly, waiting as if to buy vegetables from the last stand in the village, but really waiting to spread their legs for the enemy, who though they are very polite think older ladies are the most dangerous because they wear the most clothes and have had the most children; they could hide an entire village between their legs if they wanted to.

Farah felt nothing as she took off her clothes all the way down to naked, avoiding looking at her body whose loose flesh she rarely inspected, almost as if it belonged to someone else. The women guards poked around with rubber gloves and Farah felt nothing—no anger, nothing more than tiredness. Such things were accepted as part of life, like that woman's six miscarriages, and the one child who lived got polio and hobbled around on crutches, and that widow who had no nephews or uncles or cousins to help carry her groceries from the market—not pleasant, but unavoidable, God-given burdens.

And then it was done with and Farah was dressed and sweating now from the heat and looking for a *service* that would take her home. So many cabs and buses and *services* and hot people stuffing themselves inside.

"I'm going to the north, near Jenin," she told a driver.

"Then you will come with me, sister. I am going to Jenin as soon as we get two more passengers."

Farah stood with two men who were also waiting. It was hot, burning dry Jericho hot, but she was still numb as she wiped the sweat from her forehead with the edge of her white scarf.

"Are you going to Jenin?" called a young woman in a dress that reached to her knees. Several feet behind her were a young boy and girl and five large suitcases.

"Yes, and we will leave as soon as I load your bags and your children," said the dark-skinned driver as he walked over to get the suitcases and leaned down to squeeze the little boy's cheek.

After the driver had tied two of the suitcases to the roof and stuffed everything else in the trunk, Farah folded herself into the car, sitting by the door in the back with the woman and her children.

"What a relief to get away from that checkpoint," the young woman muttered to no one in particular.

"God give us strength to deal with these hardships," said Farah, not realizing that the woman and her children had crossed the bridge with the foreigners.

The woman didn't say anything.

Fully loaded, the car grumbled past the other *services* and onto the road. Dust flew up everywhere and the windshield was already caked thick with dead bugs and encrusted dust from previous trips.

Farah turned toward the window and closed her eyes, gripping the image of her so-young-nineteen-year-old daughter across the river with that man she didn't know, standing there like an angel with that tiny dead baby in her arms. No way to explain a death like this; it is God's will. Farah felt all the sadness she had resisted in her daughter's presence wash over her in the form of exhaustion, desperate exhaustion. In other times things were different, she thought. In those times you had other things to think about.

Farah. *Joy.* Surely her father had cursed her by giving her that name. One whose name means joy could only know misery. And what misery I have known, Farah thought to herself as the car rattled on the road home.

She remembered being sixteen years old, so much like that lovely daughter of hers, and sent off to live with her new old husband who gave her two children and fists that pounded her with welts to cover her body, welts she ignored or covered until it broke her father's heart and he convinced her husband to release her with divorce to freedom, but there is no freedom for a divorced woman with two children.

"You will marry again," her father would say, though her mother kept silent on the subject except to say, "God willing."

She did marry again, married a *service* driver who died of a disease three years and two more babies after they were wed. A disease with a name that does not translate, the doctor told her, as she stumbled hopelessly over the English pronunciation. What does it matter if I can pronounce it? If he were murdered, would I go around all day whispering the name of his killer?

A blackened widow back in her parents' house, with four giant mouths to feed and a father who said, "You will marry again," with the same frequency he recited the first chapter of the Quran, and a mother who wouldn't say more than "God willing."

The car rattled with every bump in the road.

"Were you visiting relatives in Jordan?" asked the young woman.

Farah turned to look at her, surprised by how Arab her features were in contrast to her short curly hair and her western clothes. "My daughter and her husband live there," she said, winking at the little girl who was leaning on her mother's lap, at the same time pushing the ache back behind her breast.

"Let it be God's will that they have many healthy children," the woman said, and Farah smiled but turned toward the window again.

"I've forgotten how beautiful it is," said the woman.

Farah guessed that she had been in the United States.

"Puerto Rico," she said, and when Farah raised her eyebrows she smiled and began to talk in a loud but not offensive voice. "You'd be surprised how many Arabs go to Puerto Rico. It's beautiful too, if you can close your eyes to the crime and the lack of morality." The woman rubbed her hands together in her lap and Farah looked down at the shiny red nails. "That's why I came back. How can I let my children grow up in a place where girls are women at eleven years old and boys shoot real guns at each other at twelve?"

Farah didn't say anything, but one of the men in the front seat turned around. "I lived in Puerto Rico for fourteen years and it is incredible. I even had a Puerto Rican wife and three children by her, but one morning I woke up and felt I was lying in the Devil's bed, so I came back. I asked my wife to come with me but she refused. She asked me how I expected her to let my children grow up with *petróleos,* which is what they call Arabs, as if we Palestinians have anything to do with oil. That's when I knew I had made the right decision to leave."

The driver and the other man nodded and no one spoke for a few minutes, letting the man's words marinate.

And you came home and married a virgin in the name of God, Farah thought to herself.

"Now I have a beautiful young wife who is Muslim and virtuous. I thank God for making me realize what is right," said the man.

Farah felt a surge at his words. He sounded just like her first husband, who wanted to go between the legs of a young virgin, to feel control after all those years of foreign prostitutes and cheap women. He would speak with God's words spattered on top of his own and people thought him virtuous, so virtuous he beat his own baby out of her and then beat her more and told her she was careless for letting a child die inside her very own body. Again she pushed the ache back behind her breast.

"It's very dangerous too," said the woman.

"I didn't know that," said Farah, for some reason thinking about the dog her current husband ran over by accident a couple of weeks ago, just before she crossed the river to see her daughter. It used to hang around behind their house and wasn't dangerous at all; in fact, Farah liked that it came to visit. When it was hungry, it would come by their house and bark and she would come out and throw it whatever tiny leftover scraps they had. Then it chose the wrong time to come and bark, oblivious of the van speeding toward it. Fate ran it over, but didn't kill it. Her husband left it to die and Farah found it whimpering in a pile of blood under the bushes by a tree. For some reason the sight of it made her insides ache with sadness and she patted the dog, which was too much in pain and close to dying to move more than to bare its teeth halfheartedly at her. She sat with it under the fig tree, trying to give it a couple of minutes of company before she went into the house for a knife to slit its throat and put it out of its misery. She even dug a hole to bury it, feeling such anger toward her husband that if he had come to her while she was digging, she might have hit him over the head with the shovel. *But what can you expect from a man married to a woman who has been married twice before him?*

"We had a very hard time when we were there," the woman was saying, and for a moment Farah forgot what she was talking about. "There is so much crime. Several times we were robbed at gunpoint. I lost all my gold to thieves. The houses are like prisons with built-in bars to keep the evil out, but it doesn't work; the evil comes in anyway."

The woman's son, who up to this point had been kneeling

on the seat with his head hanging out the window, was now looking at his mother, engrossed.

"There are lots of dangerous men there," he said to Farah, as if flaunting his bravery for having survived it.

"You think that's bad," said the man in the front seat. "My brother owns a liquor store and he was shot during a robbery one day. Now he is paralyzed."

There were quiet murmurs from everyone in the car, and Farah felt tired and irritated at having to be reminded of all the tragedies in her life, unable to shake the image of her father, who though not paralyzed could not move around on his own, his body shaking constantly. She had to feed and bathe him while he tripped over phrases like "you will marry again." Over and over the words came from his quivering parched lips, "You will marry again," sometimes clutching at her with hands that felt like claws and made her flinch, even though this was her father and the only man she had ever loved in her life. She washed his withered body every day, even shaved him, determined to preserve his dignity, even if it meant cleaning places a daughter should never see. Her mother certainly couldn't do the job—she couldn't do much on her own either and Farah felt a pang in her heart as she remembered the day her mother had dipped a piece of steaming bread into dish soap, thinking it was olive oil. All too much to bear. And now all of this coming back because of this man's words, as though he were trying to race his tragedy with hers.

Don't you know grief is quiet, she wanted to say, but he just kept talking.

"His wife was found to have a cancerous brain tumor and died at the age of twenty-six, leaving him paralyzed with four children to take care of."

More murmurs.

"May God give you strength to deal with these hardships," said the driver in a strong voice.

Farah found herself willing the man to be quiet, willing everyone to be quiet and vaguely wondering what the other man in the front seat was keeping tucked inside, what sad story he was being forced to remember. We have all had our tragedies, she wanted to say. Don't remind us and don't show us that your tragedies are worse. In front of God we are all equal.

She kept silent and looked out the window, wondering if her own young son was better, wondering if her parents would recognize her, if her husband had found any extra work. She said nothing, just tucked those thoughts back behind her right breast and slept, her head bouncing against the window.

She dreamed that she bore her daughter's child and that it was healthy and could recite the opening chapter of the Quran, which it did over and over again, sprinkling it every so often with "you will marry again." When the *service* came to a stop, she woke up and believed, just for a moment, that it was true.

We are from God and to Him we return, she muttered to herself as the car started up again and she watched the countryside roll by on her way home.

Fat, thick, raw silence. My mother will be sad tonight and her food will not be tasty. You can't drink these aches without spitting them out somewhere. Farah's daughter will go on to have healthy children, but Farah will bring us her tragedies, sew them under my mother's skin, and walk away; stitches as penance for an easy life.

SORAYA

7

....

VISAS

I am a new breed. A rebel. My mother and her sisters can spill a story from any woman, but I can make a man talk. I am in between. Familiar ears. Safe mouth. I have men as friends, as well as lovers.

Black leather, like cool with gold leather on the shoulders, and a little fringe like spaghetti. Droopy mustache on either side of his lips. Looks like a Mexican, I'd say, but no, like a man in charge of himself, he says.

Not typical visa entry, not like the others:

Student Visa Who Hangs Out With Arabs
Student Visa Who Hangs Around With Non-Arabs
Instant Citizen Who Came In On A Relative's Citizenship
Illegal Immigrant Who Came In On Tourist Visa And
    Never Left
Citizen By Virtue Of Marriage

After those categories come two more:

Works His Ass Off (Have to if you want to make it)
Doesn't Work A Lick (America is the Land Of
    Opportunity and should be handed to you on a silver
    platter. Besides, it's hard to get used to an 8, 10, or 12
    hour day.)

Walid doesn't fit into those categories anymore. He started out as Student Visa, then went to a new category: Student Visa Who Made Friends With Americans. He went to technical school, and now he repairs copy machines and pretty much Works His Ass Off.

He tries to avoid the Arab community because they are too expensive to be around. "Someone is always getting married, having a baby, getting a new job, and you have to spend too much money on them. I spend money on no one and no one spends money on me." That, and they are very nosy. Nosy people are like magnet and steel to each other, and Walid's mother, Um Radwan, is the nosiest woman on earth.

He's got a routine too.

At work he drives his own car because it comes out as more profitable than driving the company car.

Always looks neat, and lately, especially with the black alligator skin cowboy boots, looks just like a Mexican.

"The boots are comfortable," he says. "Besides, my mustache makes my face look longer."

His tastes aren't Mexican at all, though. Tastes are pure white man. Lives in Orange County. "Some minorities are fine, but live in an area that's all minority and you've got problems. White people are better protected, so it's better to live around them."

Every Friday he does not go to pray, but instead goes to Samson's, three blocks from his apartment, and has four beers, *just enough to carry you away.* Knows the bartender,

Greg. It's been four years since the first time he came in the place, since Greg asked him his name.

"Walid," he told him.

"How 'bout I just call you Willy," Greg the bartender said.

"I learned your language, you can learn my name," he told him.

"Fair enough."

But times got tough and Samson's closed temporarily: "Dear customers, Promise to come back soon. Just need to get some more money. We'll be back. The Management."

For a few weeks, Walid bought four beers at 7-Eleven and drank them at home, but it just wasn't the same. When I snuck out for a visit, he decided it was time to find a new haunt. "I don't like to drink and drive, so it has to be close by."

Which is how it was that five Fridays after Samson's closed temporarily, Walid and I found ourselves at The Jack Knife. It was the first time Walid had been there. White name, white customers, white neighborhood.

Twenty minutes inside and Walid got a tap on his gold shoulder.

"Speak English!" a red face shouted in whiskey breath.

Walid looked at him hard, looked into the blue eyes lost in a sea of blood vessels.

"We speak what we please," he told him quietly, not scared, but honest.

"Fucking Mexicans," said a back as soft as the eyes.

"He thinks we're Mexicans." We laughed, and Walid knew the soft man would be watching and would be thinking we were laughing at him and would not let it go.

Though he had drunk only two beers, Walid stood up and said to me in Arabic, "It is time we leave, my dear. I do not want problems and I am in no mood to fight." The whiskey-breath man, even if he had heard him, would not have understood and would just have thought that we were talking about him and would have gotten his friends together, which is what he did.

"Hey you fucking Mexicans. Chickenshit boy running away from us?"

"We've had our fill and we're leaving," replied Walid like he thought there was no problem, which he didn't.

"You speak English pretty good for a wetback. Just remember, this ain't a Mexican joint. You go somewhere else to drink your *cervezas* and hang out with your *puta*." The whiskey man and his friend crumbled in heavy laughter, still not charged enough to fight, but well on their way.

Walid held my elbow and guided me past them and out the door.

"Fucking Mexicans!"

"We're not Mexicans!" I shouted. "We're Americans."

This charged the men enough to take the ten steps it took to reach us and to swing fists into Walid's face and body. I was too surprised to do anything at first, and by the time I thought to swing, sweaty hands were gripping my wrists behind me. Walid tried to hit back, but he tried harder to get away and the original whiskey-breath man caught him and slammed his head against a light post, which made him fall. The man kicked Walid in the belly and ran away laughing just in time, seeing as it was early in a white neighborhood. The police came soon to find Walid laying in a heap on the sidewalk.

"So they beat you up for being Mexican?" the policewoman asked.

"We're not Mexican."

"You got beaten up for being Mexican and you're not Mexican? What are you?"

"Palestinian."

"Well you got off pretty lucky then." The policewoman was quiet for a minute. "That jacket sure makes you look Mexican."

Sneak back home, heart still pounding hours later, with rage, with hate. What loser morons and, squeezing tears out, wishing that it was one of those American movies where Walid would knock those guys to the floor and we would walk off without a scratch, my heroic prince defending my honor . . . but that's not what the American movie would show, would it? Instead it would show the super American guy knocking the scummy Arab flat on the ground, like what happened. Still wishing . . . that I were a superhero like in those cartoons where she comes in and wipes out the bad guys and still looks great. But there aren't any Arab ones, are there? My hair is too dark, too thick; my skin is too far away from white to let me even pretend to be an American superhero.

So I put on headphones in my too quiet California house, tuck the Walkman into my pocket, close my eyes, and dance hard until the rage begins to fade.

8

....

FLOWERS FROM MY ROZA

W hen I was younger, she used to scare me, like she was a *jinn* walking down the street. Now I know that she has a sickness, that God made her that way, just the way He made me this way. . . .

Empty girl in silence like a post, guarding what is sacred, what is not known but is known, and spoken of in hushed voices. She still stands there, by her house at the edge of the path leading down to the heart of Nawara, holding a flower, pulling the petals off one by one, waiting to eat the last one, waiting for him to leave.

"Hey, retarded girl," shouts one little boy.

Eyes vacant like space uninterrupted.

"For shame that such things happen," my mother says under her breath, as she does every time we see her. "God give the poor girl strength. And even to her mother."

And still she stands, fixed, listening, hearing, but not understanding, or understanding but not allowing any words to reach her lips, any truth to come to her eyes.

Hers is a story my mother will not discuss. Um Radwan, however, will talk about it all I want and my mother lets her go on—she is probably the only person in the village who does—maybe because she thinks it's one of those stories that needs telling and needs saving, maybe because she knows Um Radwan needs to talk.

It could have been yesterday, or it could have been forty years ago that Lubna Aziz was born possessed, retarded. Such pity we all had for her mother when one year later her husband, two sons, and parents were killed when their truck exploded after being hit by another truck. We all followed in her grieving, brought her food, sat with her, wailed, and looked after that awful daughter of hers. The elders of Nawara always set money aside for her to make sure that she and Lubna would never go hungry. Her gratitude? To stop speaking to anyone. Dignified mourning in silent black with no interruptions.

I never much cared for her, before or after her disasters. She was poorer than our family and younger than my eldest son, Radwan, and yet she refused him in marriage and made him run to America to find whores to satisfy him. She stole her own happiness as well as mine by refusing my son. Our lives could have been so different if it were not for Safa's insolence, but no one remembers that; no one thinks of her name, Safa, *untroubledness, purity,* when they call her Um Khalid for the eldest of the two boys who died. *May God have mercy on them. May God give her strength, for that is a heavy burden to bear.*

Still, she was an insolent woman before her tragedy, and she did not change in her wordless mourning. For years, on the rare occasions you would see her wandering silently through the village, she would be wearing a black *roza* without a stitch of embroidery, not a dot of red on the shoulder, nor a hint of sunshine yellow on the sleeve, nor a misplaced flower on the hem. Her grieving was somber gloom and she carried it too far, ordaining herself the village martyr. I mean, finish. We must accept the will of God, not get strangled by it. If everyone were to act as Um Khalid in the face of grief, our village would be as quiet as death itself. If every tragedy I lived through showed, I would be wailing all day long, for my dead son, may God have mercy on him, my lost sons, my dead husband, my daughter who cannot be taught the right way. Finish. This is God's will and we must accept it.

At the very least Um Khalid should have come off her mountain of self-pity for the sake of that stupid girl Lubna, as if being retarded isn't a hard enough burden to bear, but to have a mother whose ways are also retarded, now that is just too much.

It was hard to be nice to Lubna because she was such an ugly, ugly child with eyes wandering around in their sockets and a mouth that always dribbled. She even walked crooked. Worst of all, and probably because of her mother's sulking silence, Lubna never perfected talking. She could say the easy everyday things like hello, how are you, may God lift your burdens from you, say hello to your family, but beyond that— and a few odd songs that she would sing over and over and over—she tended to trip over her tongue, which spent too much time on the outside of her lips.

There were some in Nawara who took pity on her and would try to help her or feed her, especially when she was younger. I told them what fools they were to bring a clearly possessed creature into a house of healthy children—how would they know if Lubna's condition was contagious or not, or if she could hurt their children. Besides, people had problems of their own without adding to them the ugly face of a drooling retarded girl.

It was some time after my youngest son had left for the United States, and my daughter had married and moved to the city, that I first noticed a difference in Um Khalid. One day I was at Abu Khuder's vegetable stand and I saw her, though I thought maybe it wasn't her because she had embroidered strips running down the back of her dress. I didn't pay much attention to her until I heard a clear and very feminine voice speaking.

"I almost forgot to get zucchini. If you tried my stuffed zucchini, Abu Khuder, you would see that it's the best in the village."

I turned to look, not recognizing the voice, and while I couldn't see her face, from the back she looked like Um Khalid, except of course for those colorful strips on her dress. Finally she left and I went to Abu Khuder and gave him my vegetables to weigh.

"Was that Um Khalid?"

"Yes," said Abu Khuder as he put the eggplants on the scale. "She prefers to be called Um Lubna now."

"Why on earth would she want to be called Um Lubna? To be reminded of that horrible creature she brought into this miserable world?"

"Shame on you, Um Radwan. She says it makes her too sad to always remember her sons, may God have mercy on them; that she'd rather be attached to the living than the dead."

Imagine severing your son's name from you! It is shameful. Nothing has changed. She is just as insolent as ever, causing any scandal she can, doing exactly as she pleases instead of doing what is right. It is just as well she didn't marry Radwan or our family might have been carried away by her evil.

Seeing her got me to thinking about Radwan on my way home. He is my favorite son and is far away living in Los

Angeles where they have a new disaster every time I turn on
the television, but he is successful, a jeweler. A mother can be
proud of a boy who owns his own store and lives in a house
that overlooks the beach, even if he doesn't bring her for a
visit—but who would want to be troubled by such a journey
anyway.

Home and up the eleven stairs built to cause me more pain
than I already know.

"*As-salaamu alaykum,* Um Radwan."

It is my neighbor who lives in the house behind mine. We
chatted for a while, and just as I was about to continue, I
thought of Um Khalid.

"Have you seen Um Khalid lately?"

She thought for a moment, sticking an obese finger beneath the blue scarf on her head to scratch her scalp. *I'm sure
she has lice.*

"No, why?"

"I just saw her at Abu Khuder's and she was talking with
him like a young bride, telling him how she was going to cook
him stuffed zucchini and how clever she is."

"Shame on you, Um Radwan, for saying things like that
when she has so many burdens to bear."

"Swear to God. I'm not kidding. She was also wearing a
roza covered with embroidery."

"Surely you must have imagined it, Um Radwan."

Talk about insolent. I continued up the stairs without another word. How dare she talk to me as though I were losing
my mind.

A few days later, I was squatting in the garden pulling the
weeds from around a limp tomato plant when she came up
to me, looking as though she might explode.

"*As-salaamu alaykum.*"

"*Alaykum as-salaam.*"

"Um Radwan, I just came from the pharmacy and Um Khalid was there. Do you know she likes to be called Um Lubna now?"

"So now you believe me."

"She has changed so much. It was just as you said and she wore a *roza* covered with embroidery. You should have seen her chatting with the other women. They looked like schoolgirls. She is becoming the same cheerful woman she used to be before all of her tragedies."

"Why should you have doubted me?"

"Oh, Um Radwan, I'm sorry," she said, her fat finger darting underneath her scarf. "We've seen her so gloomy for so long, it seemed an impossible change. It made me very happy to see her like that. Thank God she has finally stopped mourning. Maybe Lubna will come back to normal now too." She paused and looked at my garden. Then, instead of lingering to chat as she usually does, she turned to go. "See you later, Um Radwan," she said and walked back toward her house.

"Just you wait," I said, though she was already out of earshot. "Um Lubna is up to something. Mark my words." *And surely you are not stupid enough to believe that there is hope for that poor daughter of hers.*

Not long after this, the changes in Um Lubna became obvious to everyone. She was seen more and more often around the village in outrageous *rozas* (purple and gold, pink and gray) tight around her belly with a bra underneath to keep her breasts from sagging, and she would be walking with gaiety in her step. She wrapped her hair in bright-colored scarves and secured them with strings of gold or silver coins. Most striking was that when she stopped and chatted with anyone, it was as though the twelve years of silence had not taken her words away but had only dammed them up so that now they gushed out of control, soaking whomever she spoke with.

"Does she think she is a bride?" I said to Abu Khuder as I saw her leaving his stand a few months later.

"Shame on you, Um Radwan. She has mourned for twelve years. Is it so awful that she should try happiness now?"

"There are plenty of happy women who don't feel obliged to press their breasts inside a tight dress and wrap their heads in gold or silver. Who ever heard of going to buy vegetables with your head wrapped in coins like that?"

"But Um Radwan . . ."

Soon I was not the only one who doubted her motives. Rumors started, started small and harmless and grew until they were like a boulder ready to flatten her. Someone saw Um Lubna batting her eyes at this one's eighteen-year-old son. Someone else saw her lift her dress all the way up to her knees in the middle of the market. And someone else heard her singing a love song at the butcher's, of all places.

Everyone began running around with trying-to-be-discreet questions and comments rolling off their tongues: I don't understand what Um Lubna is up to; it's like all of her sadness from before is now over, and I don't know what to say to her. Do you think she has seen a ghost? Maybe the evil eye has struck her.

If anyone asked me one of these imbecilic questions, I spoke my mind: What do you think a woman is up to when she goes around dressed like that, winking at young boys and humming love songs?

Thick-headed village.

Then I had that awful sickness for two long and completely lonely months. I put Um Lubna at the back of my mind where she belongs, did not even think about her until one afternoon I was sitting in the garden, savoring the last of the day's sun, and I saw my neighbor coming toward me with her thick lips pushing out a naughty smile.

"Um Radwan, you are not going to believe what I heard. I was at the butcher's and he asked if I had any news and I said no, only that I was so happy to see Um Lubna acting normal again, and he started laughing. I asked him why he was laughing like that and wasn't he glad to see her shed her cloak of mourning and he laughed again. Then he told me not to tell anyone, but said that Abu Khuder went to Um Lubna's house to repair a window and finished his business."

"What does that mean?"

"I mean, he finished his business," she said, gesturing with her hand in such a way that there was no mistaking her meaning.

"You see. Didn't I tell you that she was up to something?"

Whose lies are these?

The next day—it was high time I got out of my sickbed—I went to the butcher's. "You know," I said to him, "it's been a while since I last saw Um Lubna. I hope she is all right. Have you seen her lately?" See what a clever way I have to ask him. As though I had no idea of what he knows.

A disgusting smile came to his face as his knife cut through a leg of lamb, and I figured he was the one starting such stories.

"I haven't seen her personally, but you might ask Abu Khuder."

"Why Abu Khuder?" I asked.

The butcher stopped a moment.

"Has Abu Khuder seen her?" I asked.

"Well, I am only repeating what he told me. He said that she came to him at his shop with that retarded girl of hers and told him that she had a window that got broken and needed repairing and asked if he could come and do it. He told her he would come at lunchtime when the shop was closed." He paused a moment to sneeze. He is a disgusting man and the spray from his sneeze showered the leg of lamb he was cutting. "So Abu Khuder went that day to repair the window and finished his business."

I looked at him, at his disgusting smile and his puffy red face and waited for him to continue. "I bet he goes back again tomorrow to see what other windows need fixing!" Laughter louder than his sneeze exploded from the depths of his stomach.

"May God punish you for speaking this way," I said, and left the store, without taking the lamb I had asked him to prepare for me.

My heart often aches, though whether it is because of my dead son, may God have mercy on him, because of my other sons who all live in the United States, because of my difficult daughter, or because of sickness, I don't know. I am an old woman with no children or grandchildren here to care for or who will care for me. One afternoon my heart ached so much that my daughter took me to a European doctor in the city and he told me that I needed to walk.

"But I do walk, doctor. I walk everywhere." Did he think we are so modern we drive down the road to buy vegetables?

"I mean you must walk for exercise."

I laughed at him, but my daughter agreed. "If he tells you that you should walk for exercise, then I think you should listen to him because it is dangerous for the body to get lazy. It's not such a strange thing to do. There are many people here who walk for exercise."

My daughter is very modern. She and her husband have an apartment in the city, she works, and she wears western clothing. I objected to all of these decisions, but eventually became used to them—what choice did I have?—just as I eventually became used to the idea of walking.

Because my house is so empty, I often wake up early, usually before sunrise and it seemed that if I were going to walk for exercise, this would be the time to do it, away from nosy and bothersome neighbors. At first it was very difficult and made my heart ache more, but as my daughter encouraged me—sometimes she would even come and stay with me on weekends and join me on my walks—I continued and soon I looked forward to it. I can't explain why I enjoy it so much, other than to say that it makes me feel a kind of peace I have not known in some time. I enjoyed it even when my back hurt, which it no longer does thanks to my generous son, Radwan, who sent me a pair of gigantic white shoes that make me tall, as though I were walking on clouds.

I usually walk up the hills on the northern side of the village, which is where Um Lubna's house is, just below the uppermost crest that overlooks the village. There are two ways to get there—I believe it is the loveliest spot in the village—the roadway that leads around Nawara and to the top directly, and the pathway, which eventually cuts through Um Lubna's property. I always take the roadway instead of the path because the footing is better and the view is lovelier.

That morning the air was clear like water, with only a hint of diesel. The wind was strong and blowing against me, making it difficult to walk up the hill. If it were not for the sweater and pants I wore under my *roza,* I would have been very cold, as it was still early. I even had to tie my scarf tightly around my head so it wouldn't blow away.

Because of the effort in fighting the wind, I was tired and I walked slowly, my cheeks beaten by the cold air. I was more than halfway up the hill, when I couldn't go any farther. I stepped a few feet off the road and sat down to rest under an olive tree that was just across from Nadia Sulayman's house.

Nadia is a very good housekeeper, and just as the inside of her house could not be cleaner, neither could the outside be lovelier. All around the house are rosebushes, and she tends them so well that they produce the biggest, brightest roses you have ever seen, purples and yellows and reds, the likes of which no one else in all of Nawara possesses.

"It is the special fertilizer my son sends from America," she says.

"She has the whole bush imported," my daughter says with contempt, or jealousy.

Whatever the reason, her roses are beautiful.

I don't know how long I had been there, when I saw ugly Lubna Aziz, dressed in one of her mother's ugly, show-off *rozas,* walking up the hill in her sideways falling way. Lubna walked slowly, like a wounded dog, and then stopped for a moment in front of a glorious purple rosebush. In a movement as smooth as bread in olive oil, she pulled her hands from her pockets, and cut a rose from the bush. In a blink it vanished into the pocket of her *roza* and she continued walking up the steep road in the direction of her house.

The smoothness of her act struck me as incredible. I was still not really rested as I got up from my spot and walked up the hill behind Lubna, who then pulled the flower out of her *roza* and was sniffing it. It looked as though she were eating a sandwich.

The wind brought me her song:

> *Everyone else drives around in cars*
> *While my grandfather rides a mule . . .*

Crazy girl with a crazy song. Why is she awake and wandering around at this hour? Surely she doesn't have a European doctor who is prescribing walks for her.

I couldn't catch up with her, so I called out to her, "*Assalaamu alaykum.*"

She turned and looked at me and then stopped, waiting for me to reach her.

"Hello, Lubna. I got very tired. That hill gets steeper every day."

She looked at me with blank eyes. "God keep you strong," she said and looked at her feet.

"Lubna, what are you doing out here so early?" She wasn't wearing socks or even a sweater under her dress. "It's much too cold for you to be out here without socks. Go inside and keep warm."

She was silent for a moment, still staring at her feet, maybe so I wouldn't have to look at her ugly face, and then in a tiny, slow voice she said, "My mother told me to come out."

"I'm sure she'd rather you were inside where it was warm."

"But I can't go back until I see the man leave."

"What man?"

"The man who makes my mother giggle."

"What man?"

"The man," she said, looking up, her eyes fighting to focus on something. "The man who fixes things."

I felt a wave of pity as I stared at this gnarled little creature, her body shivering naked underneath her dress. "Why don't you come back down with me?"

"I can't," she said and turned toward her house.

Poor ugly retarded girl. I watched her walk home and then I turned and walked up to the top of the hill and sat underneath the mulberry tree, just above Lubna's house and overlooking all of Nawara. Poor ugly retarded girl. What man makes your mother giggle? Crazy girl. Crazy stories. And I am feeling so sleepy.

"Good-bye," said a man's voice from below and my eyes popped open. Am I dreaming, or do I see Abu Khuder walking down the path toward the village? And the sun is just barely up. I fold myself so no one will see me.

And then Lubna standing with her same purple flower, plucking off the petals; at the last one, she pulled it off and shoved it in her mouth. After a moment, she spat it on the ground and started yelling, "Poison, he hates you! Poison!"

Her mother ran outside and yelled and cursed. "Shame on you! Shame, shame on you!"

Dumb girl doesn't even struggle, just falls into her mother's arms. I am so sleepy and I have seen too much and now we have this kind of woman in Nawara. It is too much ugliness, but I am too old to get involved in these scandals. Do you know that she ruined that walk for me—how can I look for lovely views when I have to worry I may see a scandal occurring in front of my very eyes?

My mother says that talking about Lubna is like stopping to stare when you go by an accident. I see that more with Um Radwan and her fantasy world where her kids are perfect. When people talk to her, they beg for stories of her kids, just so they can laugh at the lies she believes. Soraya says that Radwan, the oldest, has a tiny jewelry booth in another store on the beach where crazy men and naked women spend their time, and that he lifts weights all day to make his muscles big. She says that Walid, the next son, tries so hard to be a white man that she can't talk to him anymore. The next son is dead, and the youngest . . . no one knows how he will turn out.

But people don't laugh too loud, because they know somewhere in her has to be grief as large as anyone's, and one day it is likely to come out.

9

SCHOOL

I am the only one of my cousins who has year-round school.

Mr. Napolitano, my social studies teacher, makes fun of everyone's name. He calls me DJ. It makes me laugh. He expects me to know more than the other kids because my parents are not American, though there are lots of other kids in the class who aren't American themselves. I want to scream at him that I am just as American as anyone here.

Ma and I have the same argument, only she gets really mad: "You are Palestinian," she says in Arabic.

"*You* are Palestinian," I tell her in English. "I am American."

"You are Palestinian and you should be proud of that."

"Ma, I can't speak Arabic right, I've never even been there, and I don't like all of those dancing parties. I like stories and movies. I can be American and still be your daughter."

"No! No daughter of mine is American."

We have this fight all the time. She is always telling Baba how shameful it is that I don't speak my language, that I don't mind her, and that I walk like a boy. I sort of like the boy part of what she says, because those girls are so silly—always brushing their hair and listening to music. I hate dancing in front of all those people. My boy cousins are more fun, but I'm not supposed to play with them anymore because I am getting too old.

Baba sometimes especially likes me because I'm his only daughter. (Mina and Monia are from Ma's first husband.) He used to let me sit with him and his friends, even when Ma wanted me to help her in the kitchen. I liked to listen to their stories and when they yell at each other about politics, even though they are all on the same side. But now I'm older and I have to cut vegetables.

I have a friend at school, but I don't tell my parents about him. His name is Michael and he's Jewish, but the real problem is that he's a boy and I'm not supposed to be friends with boys. He's very funny. When I first met him I forgot his name and called him David. I was so embarrassed, but then he called me Fatima and we were even.

"My grandmother is dying," I told him one day.

"That's sad," he said. We were both quiet. "My grandmother died," he said, the way he might say he saw such and such movie.

"I'm sorry," I told him.

"Thank you, but that is not the point of my story. We went to my uncle's house to pray for her. Did you know Jews face Jerusalem when they pray?"

I didn't know that. Michael likes to bring up the similarities between Muslims and Jews, I think to show that we can be friends. I just try to forget all those things and listen to his stories.

"I didn't either. It's funny, because if you were in Jerusalem, a Muslim and a Jew would face different directions, but by the time they come to America, it's all just east. So there we were at my uncle's house and we were supposed to face east, so we all faced the television and prayed, and I thought to myself, are we praying to the television god for my grandmother's soul? I mean, she never missed her soap opera, but really!"

See what I mean about him being funny?

HALA

10

....

WHITE

I feel a mixture of relief and fatigue to be back. So many relatives and neighbors coming to pay their respects, to visit my grandmother's memory. I know they see me with curious eyes. I left before marrying age. I have finished high school and I should be coming back for marriage, not for death. I should have longer hair. I should wear makeup. I should not wear blue jeans and "extremely unfeminine dresses," as Aunt Suha says. I should stop using English words. Nila, one of my classmates at the American school, just married and is already pregnant.

~~I am unconnected.~~

There *is* comfort to be in my own house, to wake up in my own language, but all those faces I've carried with me for so long wear suspicion in their eyes as they greet me. I have walked so far away from them.

I wake up less groggy at the beginning of my second week home. Until now, time has been a blur of memories and nightmares. The pungent smell of coffee fills the air and I find Latifa in the kitchen. I open the refrigerator and there are seven whiskey bottles filled with water.

"Are you hungry?" she asks me and I am starving, but the house is beginning to close in on me so I say no.

"We'll have coffee on the porch," she says as I watch her pull the pot from the heat, one, two, and three times before it boils over. "I always know just when to pull it away," she says and sets the pot and two demitasses on the tray.

The sun is bounding in the living room, and even though the doors and windows are open the house smells of being closed up for a long time. We go to the front porch, which has no furniture except for two chairs and a small table. Everything is white. The house is white, the yard is white tile, and the six-foot wall that borders the house is white. White, white, white to blind the morning sun, as though they were in competition.

My sister is the color of the soil under the peach trees after they have been watered, which is one reason why she doesn't like me: I am lighter than she is.

She goes back in the house and returns a few minutes later with a tray of melon, bread, and cheese. "Breakfast," she announces as though I might have thought it was shoes or saddles if she had not said otherwise.

We eat without speaking. Latifa is watching me, chewing her food loudly. It occurs to me that Latifa and I share nothing, except our mother.

"You seem different," she says finally. "You don't look like you think you're better than us anymore."

"I never thought I was better. Why would you think that?"

"Because you were like that before," Latifa says. I look away and can hear her tongue lapping up crumbs on her lips and teeth. I have never been able to watch her eat. "Maybe Mama's death made you humble. It made Baba humble and you are just like him."

Latifa's words don't make me angry. It's as if I am watch-

ing two people talking as they face a white wall, but I have
no connection to them.

"Do you miss her?" I ask.

"I miss her like someone took my hands. But it's God's
will. What can you do?"

We are quiet.

Latifa is watching me. "I know you want to ask and I will
tell you now because we are sisters. When you left, I did
know she was going to die."

Like someone has taken my breath.

"Why didn't you tell me?"

"It was what Mama wanted. She was right. Things were
bad here and you did not belong in the middle of it. She
cursed you, in a way, by putting you in the American school.
Mama gave you her desires, but you have Baba's will, so
you will get them to come true for you." Latifa pauses and
breathes heavily. "Would you have gone if you had known?"

"No."

"That is why I didn't tell you. Will you stay now? Baba
thinks you will, but I know you're going back to go to the
university. You've been accepted; that means you should go."

"I don't know," I say, because I really don't.

The morning sits between us.

"Thank you," I whisper, but Latifa is studying the dregs
in her coffee cup and does not seem to have heard me.

The morning passes and I am still in a dream, though it
now is as stark as the white wall that blinds me.

11

....

WEDDINGS

*L*ater, we go into the living room and Latifa rewinds the videotape that's sitting on top of the television. "Jalal's wedding was beautiful. Bad enough you didn't come for the wedding—I can't believe you haven't seen the video. You are such a bad sister."

"It was only a couple of months ago! I had finals. And no one sent me a copy. Maybe you are the bad sister."

"It was especially wonderful since it was held in Nawara and the whole village came. How lucky we were to all have gotten permission." She says this last part like it was rehearsed. I know she hates going to my mother's village. "It's a shame you missed it."

I sit back to eat the peach I took from the fruit bowl. I used to think my father put some sort of magic in the roots of the trees to make the peaches delicious—I would eat them until they made me sick.

Modern pop music starts before a picture appears and the television vibrates. A field of wildflowers wanders across the screen on top of which my brother and his bride, Jawahir Sulayman, are superimposed. Fancy video. The camera zooms in on the happy couple and creates a heart shape around them, while the field of flowers dances behind them. Jalal looks proud as he stands stiffly in his tuxedo. I cannot read any emotion on Jawahir's face as she stands next to her new husband in a white, very western, bridal gown.

Peach juice drips down my arm.

Now we are watching the *henna* day. Jawahir sits rigidly on her throne (a decorated chair on a decorated table). Her hair is twisted elegantly on her head and she is dressed in a fancy *roza* while two women paint *henna* designs on each of her hands. The fat one is my aunt Sahar, who was the sister my mother trusted completely. "She is like a clam, only no one will ever get to the pearl, not even with a rock." Everyone says Mawal is the same. She even looks just like her mother—almost as fat. They both have a calm about them, which must be why people come to tell them what is on their minds.

When they finish the *henna,* the bride holds her palms out for everyone to see: two little hearts linked together and surrounded by delicate twisted vines and flowers. The old women begin to chant and call for her to dance. Hands reach up to help her down. As soon as she is on the floor, the music begins and she starts her dance. She is the picture of a traditional bride—a competent, but not excellent, dancer. Her shakes and twists are simple and her eyes are lowered. When she is done the other women join in.

Everybody who attended the wedding talks about my cousin Soraya's performance during this part, so I am not surprised when she appears. She is wearing a tight black dress that reaches below her knees. Her long, lush hair is loose and swinging about as she shakes her hips. Her movements are the kinds you see belly dancers make in Egyptian movies, coordinated to such a degree that she can move around the floor while her hips guide her. She is the opposite of Jawahir. Each provocative twist and shake seems to invite the viewer to watch more closely. She stares at the camera with heavily made-up eyes, no smile on her full lips.

People say vicious things about Soraya and what she does. I think it's because she does the things people are scared of. She makes me sad, and whenever I see her, I feel as though something bad is going to happen to her.

Soon the dancers are old women who sing almost forgotten songs—this is cut into briefly by men singing different almost forgotten songs and dancing the *dabka;* their dance is separate but simultaneous.

Latifa is dancing gracelessly in a blue sequined dress. "My dress cost three hundred and fifty dollars," she shouts, as though we were not sitting next to each other. When I say nothing, she tries another topic. "Look at Soraya. Can you believe she dances like that with no shame?"

I watch Soraya some more. My mother knew Soraya when she was very young, and even then she said it was as though Soraya had been touched by something magical—in both a good and a bad sense. Her own mother, Maysoun, stopped trying to fight it, just showed her disappointment to everyone, even though it seemed as though it came from within, and was not something that could be controlled.

All eyes are on Soraya.

"She is a beautiful dancer," I say, though I know this will irritate Latifa even more.

"She is shameful."

I look back at Jawahir, who is once again sitting on her throne, staring off into space. Surely this is not what my father has in mind for me. Marriage, marriage, marriage. This is not what I want from my life. I've seen what happens when very young girls marry men they don't know.

"Don't do anything you don't want to" were Aunt Fay's so American last words at the airport, also aware that marriage was probably what my father was thinking when he called me to come home.

I used to try to imagine Latifa married, wondering if it perhaps would have spared her some misery. She would make the perfect traditional bride: ready to follow orders, ready to serve. There is something so distant about her, though. Is there any man who could be happy with that?

And who could my father want me to marry? When I was home the last time, he had Hossam, Aunt Suha's son, in mind. I would not, and will not, marry my first cousin.

I am not ready to marry at all. I know this. And if I stay here, I might come to feel differently. And then I will be like my mother, The Woman Of Unfulfilled Dreams. Better to be like Uncle Hamdi, The Voice Of Reason And Capitalism. If I stay I will be one of my father's jokes too. A joke that makes nobody laugh.

But my father must know by now that he will lose me forever if he pushes too hard. I am not willing to stay and take that chance; I realize that now. I will iron smooth my thoughts, try to be patient and kind and see what is in store for me. I have faith that he will do what is right, having already lost so much . . . and so while I remain unconnected, like a charm without a chain to hang from, I am happy.

SORAJA

12

IRONIC

SUCCESS

Sameer Samaha, Um Radwan's third son. His story is the saddest Nawara story I know. I knew him quite well, perhaps better than anyone. He was my father's relative and he lived with us when he first came from Nawara.

Everybody liked him because he kept to himself and didn't get in other people's business. People said that he had a white heart, which means it's clean and good. I liked him, and he liked to talk to me and to my mother about his life and his dreams. Sameer came to this country to be a success story, not millionaire success, but a place here and a house in Nawara and lots of kids and enough money to be a happy kind of success. That's not my fantasy, but that's what so many people want, mostly men, and mostly older men; they don't usually talk like that when they are in their teens or twenties. Sameer was different from most of the guys who come from Nawara. He never seemed to get distracted by glittery Los Angeles, but he didn't judge it, either. He worked for my dad with his businesses and also in our grocery store. He never argued about the long hours he had to work, or the low pay I'm sure he got, or even about how boring it was. He always said that he knew he would be something if he worked hard for it.

Things are never what you think they're going to be. Our loud loud neighborhood got on his last nerve because the music, the shouting, or the police cars would keep him up at night, and he was already tired. I am so glad we don't live in that neighborhood anymore. He got to be like everyone else, who learns to take it, or leaves. He took it, and covered his irritation by doing more work, which my parents really liked.

Something else that made him so different from everyone else was that he didn't spend money. Hardly anything.

He came when he was nineteen or twenty, or something, and he went to work during the day and part of the evening, and he slept in our house. That was his life. Boring. I liked having him around, because he was so normal and nice and not gossipy or obnoxious like some of our relatives. Sometimes he would give money to my mother to help out with the household expenses, which of course she loved—even though we were not suffering for money. She would save it for him and buy him clothes, or cologne, or things she thought he needed, because he would never buy anything for himself. ("That's because his mother spoiled him so much, he didn't know how to buy himself anything," my mother explained.) Sometimes he would make the biggest fuss, like if my mother got him some fancy shirt or something, and she would have to lie and say she got it for Dad or for Tariq on sale, that it didn't fit them, and that she couldn't return it. He was so weird about money. My mother used to beg me to be like him, even if it was just for a week.

Every week when he was paid, he put all but twenty dollars into a bank account. "This is for the future," he would tell us.

My dad would argue constantly with Sameer. "Supposing you die tomorrow?" he would say.

"Only God knows what is in store for us. I am making the best effort I can for the sake of my future. Besides, I don't plan to live like this until I'm eighty, just until I have enough saved up to go home and marry."

Everyone teased him about his saving, and about his trusting banks to keep his money, and for being so serious, but really everyone liked Sameer and respected him for his determination—especially my dad, which meant a lot to him since his own dad died when he was young. My dad is a really hard worker, in a kind of different way, but they respected each other.

Five years after he started working in the grocery store and in Dad's businesses, Sameer moved out of our house, put a down payment on a house—a house here in Los Angeles!—and returned to Nawara with his savings to look for a bride.

Wild. Some men can't do that even if they have been working here all their lives.

No one knew how much money he had saved, but everyone knew that he was a rich man. He went home and, together with his busybody mother, went to the house of Suad Madani. I didn't remember her very well, but I know she was very pretty. I do remember my mother talking about the women in that family, and she said they were all headstrong and selfish, and that it was not a good match. He was the type who wanted a doting wife, and this wife would be the type to want control of her life.

"While I don't agree with its necessity, my daughter is determined to finish her schooling, and I will not force her to marry against her will," her father told them.

"I have been in America for a long time," Sameer said with such pomp that Suad's father laughed. "I know that a woman must be happy on her own for a man and a woman to be happy together. If Suad wants to continue with her studies, she is welcome. There is plenty of money, a community college near to the house I bought where she can take classes, and all my support to do what she wishes. After all, if she is happy so am I."

I remember Suad's father pretty well. He was one of those people you always saw who walked heavy and quiet, who kept his thoughts to himself. He made his money—and destroyed his health—by working in the quarries. He, like every other parent, did not wish that life on his children, so he accepted Sameer's proposal on his daughter's behalf.

Sameer did not know until later that Suad had cried and screamed and starved herself for three days in protest against her father's decision. She told him this one evening as they sat next to each other on the sofa, watching their wedding video.

"I would not have married you if I had known you were against it."

"I know that now," she told him.

Sameer leaned over and kissed his young bride. He was absolutely in love with her. Everyone told him that love came in time, but he felt it from the first time he saw her with her pale, pale skin and her huge eyes. "I love you," he whispered in her ear and was so overcome by emotion he almost started to cry.

"I love you too," she answered.

He picked up her little body and carried her to the bedroom without bothering to turn off the video.

I know these things because he used to confide in my mother, and sometimes I could hear them. It was like he wanted to make sure he was doing everything right.

"I want to be a good husband, Maysoun," he would say. "Tell me what I need to do."

Too bad this story didn't end like that, where everyone is happy and doing the right thing.

Honeymoons don't last forever. Sameer was back to working long days: ten hours, twelve hours, fifteen hours. He would usually go home for lunch, and in the beginning he would try to stay, but as time passed, my dad had more and more for him to do. On the days when he didn't come home at lunch, he would come home in the evening with some little present for her, a candy, a flower, a stuffed animal. But over time he stopped doing that too.

He adored her. All day long he thought of her as he boxed and unboxed and shelved and swept and accepted money from people whose language he still had difficulty understanding.

Suad began taking English classes and Sameer was relieved that she had something to do all day while he was gone. On her way home she would stop by the grocery store and he would sit with her. When the weather was nice, which was almost always, they sat on milk crates together and drank sodas, or they would sit together in the little back room. It was really sad because it was so obvious that he loved her way more than she loved him. So many times I saw them sitting together, with him looking at her all lovey-dovey like in a music video, and her looking away into the distance with God-knows-what thoughts in her mind.

I used to tell my mother, but she didn't see it. I think some of the problem was that Suad was a very smart girl, and even though Sameer was so nice and all, he wasn't that brilliant. Maybe what my mother and all those ladies had been calling "headstrong" for generations was really just women being smarter than the men they were married to. Nobody really knew Suad or was close with her. She would talk sweet in everyone's face, say all the right things, but who knows what she was thinking, one of those people who show one face outside her house and another one inside.

Sameer would watch Suad leave, watch her thin ankles and imagine them carrying her home, imagine them supporting her as she cooked so that when he came home at 10:45, there would be a delicious meal waiting for him. He imagined her watching television, or a wedding video, or listening to music, or dancing, or talking on the phone with this cousin or that aunt. He would fill his mind with these thoughts for as long as he could and it would keep him awake until 10:45, which was when he always returned home.

I know she made Sameer happy. He would say that he knew God had granted him a lot and he knew there was hard work ahead of him, but he also knew he was going in the right direction, which I guess is how it was that he managed to ignore the signs of disaster that wandered in front of him.

Sameer and Suad had been married for three years—he had been in this country for eight—when he really began talking to my mother, and sometimes me when Dad was not around. I think he thought my dad would think it was unmanly that he was asking a woman how he should deal with his wife.

He talked about everything, like how they hardly ever had sex and that's why there were no children on the way. Of course, she cooked his meals, but usually she wouldn't wait up for him anymore and he ate alone.

Sometimes he would come to our house just to ask my mother for advice. He worried that Suad was unhappy because she still had not gotten pregnant. He thought that perhaps this was why she was so distant. He tried to comfort her, but it seemed that whatever he did irritated her, and so he tried to keep quiet, to leave her alone if that's what she wanted. From everything I heard him say, I figured that Suad was making fun of him, like she had a private joke going.

One night, he came home after they closed the grocery.

(Sameer and Tariq would stand guard for Dad while he carried out the day's cash. They brought the cars right up to the front door and stood facing the street, their hands on their guns, until Hussein was safely in his Cutlass and drove away. They have to do that every night. If someone were to come along and rob them, they would get thousands of dollars.)

So he's telling Ma how every once in a while Suad waited up for him, maybe hoping for some affection, maybe just wanting a little company. Sameer tried to be chatty with her on these occasions, but usually he had eyes for nothing except dinner and bed. Sometimes if Suad was awake when he came home, she would rub his feet or his back.

So that night he walked through the door at 10:45 just like always. He was tired and had an odd, empty feeling, like at the store after all those people have left and there's no one left to thank you for being the only ones brave enough to open a grocery store in that neighborhood. Poor guy, he was probably starting to see life for what it was and to realize that no grand prizes were around the corner waiting for him.

Suad was awake that night, very awake, and was wearing a pink satin, very short nightgown. Something struck him as odd, but he was too tired to put his finger on just what it was.

"Welcome home," she said with a cup of tea in her hand.

"Welcome home to you," he said, kissing her on the lips. "Are you all dressed up for me?"

"No, I've been entertaining," she answered, smiling.

He laughed, but didn't feel quite right. Then he followed her into the kitchen.

"I made stuffed zucchini today," she said, opening the refrigerator. "I hope you like it."

"Of course I'll like it. Didn't you make it?" He was delighted by her friendliness.

She put the plate she had prepared for him in the microwave. "How was work?"

"Same, same, same." He didn't continue the conversation because the microwave bell went off. He could see how thin she still was, not like most girls whose figures transformed completely as soon as they got married.

"Enjoy it," she had said and put the plate in front of him.

I used to feel so embarrassed for him for the things he told Ma, who would try to tell him in a roundabout way what a woman needed and wanted. That kind of grossed me out, listening to her. So that night he said they made love, unlike most nights when he came home exhausted and she didn't want to. He would always tell her, "Tomorrow, my dear. Tomorrow I will have more energy and you will be happy."

And then tomorrow would come and go and if he wasn't tired, she would be asleep or on her period. She didn't complain to him about not having sex, which seemed weird to me too.

Then at 5:30 A.M. he was up again, made coffee and was back to open the grocery at 6:00.

I know this city can get to anyone with its ugly sidewalks, even in summer, and everywhere trash that chases you home. There were days when Sameer had difficulties because he was so tired, and it got into him and he couldn't shake it. He was only fifteen blocks from home, and still he wouldn't go except at lunchtime and at 10:45 when the day was finally over. He was so predictable. No sneaking, no suspicions.

Then one day—I was at the store that day—he was sweeping out front, when a man came dressed in a tuxedo and carrying a pile of sharp red roses. So out of place in that neighborhood, even though we are in California and weird things happen. The man stood in front of the building next to our store, right under one of the windows, and called out. "Rosaria. Rosaria. Where are you, my love?"

I was standing at the door with Ma just as Rosaria, with curlers on her head, came to the window. Rosaria came into the store and hung around outside so much that I knew all about her troubled love stories.

"Aye, Constantine, what are you doing here?"

"What am I doing here?" he asked with exaggerated shock spicing his gravely voice. He turned to us. "What am I doing here?" Then he turned back to her. "Rosaria, isn't it obvious? I've come to ask you to marry me."

Rosaria had no words. She stared at him. I remember this like it was yesterday. She touched her hair and remembered the curlers.

"Aye, how can you ask me to marry you when I have curlers in?"

Constantine turned to the small crowd that had gathered with us. "How can I ask her to marry me with curlers on her head?" He turned back to Rosaria and walked closer to the building. "Rosaria, you can have curlers in your hair from now until the day we die and I will still love you."

Rosaria held her hands together over her heart and started to cry.

"So what's the answer, Rosaria?" someone yelled from the other side of the store.

"Yea, what's the answer?" shouted Sameer, who was delighted like a child. I know he liked Rosaria, despite her foul mouth.

"My answer? Constantine, my answer is yes!"

"Yeah!" we all shouted, and everyone clapped and made noises.

"Now open that door and let me kiss you before my lips fall off my mouth from desire," said Constantine. I swear that's exactly what he said: "before my lips fall off from desire." Before he went in the building he turned to us and bowed. "Wish me luck."

Everyone cheered again.

Sameer went back to work with the thought of Constantine and Rosaria in his head and couldn't keep from smiling. "That will keep me happy for the rest of the day," he told us. I guess you could call Sameer a romantic type.

Anyway, he had been working in the back for a while when suddenly he came up to us and told us he would like to leave—it couldn't have been later than five in the afternoon and maybe even earlier. When Ma asked why, he said the strangest thing.

"I have to kiss my wife," he said. "I have to love her and make her feel loved. I will treat her American-style, with no hiding words."

Even Ma was surprised, but of course she said yes.

"Don't worry, I will be back in time for closing."

"Tariq can come. Don't worry about coming back. We'll see you tomorrow."

"Thank you. Good-bye, Maysoun. Bye, Soraya."

We watched him leave the store and practically run down the ugly, all-year-round-stinking sidewalks filled with children and broken bottles. He was walking like he had a giant secret inside him and would explode if he did not give it to his wife immediately.

That look on his face as he was running off was so happy and excited, like a little kid. Who could have known what would happen?

We figured out the rest of the story later. What they told us was that as he got to his house, Suad was sitting on the front stoop and as he started to go up the path toward her, a man grabbed him from behind and asked for his money. Suad said that Sameer refused to give him his wallet, that he hesitated, which made the mugger angry. He made horrible threats and waved a knife in front of his face.

Suad says Sameer still refused and told him to get out of

there. The man asked again, and again Sameer refused. Then the man stabbed him, fourteen times, on his face, his stomach, and his hands, which the police told us meant he put up quite a fight.

Suad was screaming and screaming and eventually the police came, but Sameer was dead by then. Suad went crazy, screaming at everyone and no one could understand her. We didn't see her until we went to the hospital later on.

Suad told the police that the man who did it was a short, very muscular Latin man who wore a sweatshirt with a hood so she did not see his face.

For days Ma couldn't eat. I was just angry. Ma didn't want to go back to work, because she said the killer probably had come and bought something from us, and she would always wonder if the person she was selling to was the person who killed Sameer. She changed her attitude when she finally went back and so many people from the neighborhood brought flowers, and candles, and ladies were crying with her.

It's different for me too. I don't believe Suad's story. I think she had something to do with it.

Lots of things don't make sense. First, Suad says she was sitting on the stoop outside when Sameer came. She would never sit outside for no reason, and she wasn't waiting for him because she didn't know he was coming home that early. Second, if you were a mugger and saw a girl sitting on a stoop wearing gold bracelets up to her elbows, wouldn't you choose her to rob before you robbed some guy who didn't look like he had a lot of money? Besides, the police say that most muggers are drug addicts. If Suad couldn't see his face because of the hood, chances are neither could Sameer, since he came behind him, so why would a mugger murder someone who couldn't identify him? Stab him fourteen times? In broad daylight? The guy must have been covered in blood and someone would have had to notice. Third: Sameer would not argue; Sameer would hand over the money. Maybe if Suad had said that the mugger got mad because Sameer only had ten dollars, maybe then I wouldn't think it so weird. He was so crazy over her that he would have cut off his hand and given it to the guy before he risked her safety.

Ma thinks I'm crazy, but I'm sure she had a lover. That would explain her sexy nightgown that night. Maybe she really had been "entertaining." And maybe she was entertaining the day Sameer was killed—maybe Sameer caught them. She had nothing to keep her in the house. No children, no tough husband, no close relatives. Just Suad and this sleazy city. She could have been doing anything.

After Sameer's body was sent home, Suad sold the house and moved in with her aunt and uncle in Las Vegas, of all places. She refused to go home—not even for the burial of her husband. *Haram.* What could be more shameful than that?

So that is what you get for Working Your Ass Off and then trying to be traditional.

13

AMERICA

*Y*ou would think our village was in love with America with all the people who have left, like America is the best relative in the world that everyone has to visit. America is more like a greedy neighbor who takes the best out of you and leaves you feeling empty.

After what happened to Auntie Huda, Sitti hated America, even as she watched all her other children go off and live there.

"No matter what our difficulties, it is better here," she would always say. No one would disagree either, except maybe Uncle Hamdi, "who can't sit still when he comes home. Walks around like he has worms in his toes."

Sitti would always take the worst stories and make them true for everyone. "Are we to mourn the death of our children in America just like Um Radwan? God keep such hardships far from us."

What people only whisper about is the good that has come from all the leaving: money. And this reminds me of when Sitti used to tell me stories. . . .

It was not so long ago and it was every evening.

"Sitti, Sitti, tell me a story."

My grandmother would shake out her legs and then fold them up again.

Sit down, my child, and I will tell you a story that will make you laugh. It is a story from just before your lifetime. Come here, sit close to me, but first bring me that dish of figs that your mother picked this morning. There is nothing more delicious in the world than a fresh fig.

Thank you. Now, come sit closer to me, Mawal, and let me tell you this story, for it has been on my mind and I want to remember it.

Once upon a time, a long time ago, well, actually it was not so long ago, on a Friday morning. . . . Who could have known how different that day would be from the hundreds of other Friday mornings in Nawara? The reason? Our mosque.

No, not the only mosque. You have seen that old mosque, my dear. Hundreds of years ago, that was the center of the village, and until that Friday when the mosque that Karim Sulayman had paid for to be built was opened, if anyone wanted to pray in a mosque, he had to climb up the narrow, overgrown paths and trip down rocky slopes to reach the west corner of the south hill. . . .

Yes, my child, near where the settlements are now. It is such a tiny mosque, and so undistinguished. It didn't even have a minaret and it must have been there since the time of the Prophet, God bless him and grant him salvation.

No, no one uses it now. Those who live on the settlements have no interest in old mosques, but that is another story and let's not spoil a good story with such an ugly one. Now, where was I?

Oh yes. Well, as you know, this village has changed a lot

over the years. I remember before the Catastrophe, when I was a young girl and just married, Nawara was a village of farmers. Everyone had sheep and goats and land to cultivate and satisfaction from these things. As the years passed and the changes our country was suffering began covering us with their tentacles, many young men realized that not only would they not have a future if they were to remain and work on the land or follow in their father's trade, as was expected of them, but that they might not survive at all. Certainly this was especially true in the fifties and sixties when there was a huge exodus of men who went abroad not just to become wealthy, but to survive.

I am sure that every man who left Nawara was sure that he would go, work for some years, and then have enough money that he could come home and farm his land and live in peace until he died.

You are very wise, my girl, maybe wiser than even your old grandmother. Very few men came back at all, or if they did they couldn't stay, as I'm sure you know by the number of cousins you have who don't live here. Most of the young men from Nawara who went abroad went to America, some to study but most to work in any kind of job they could find.

I know they missed the smell of coffee brewing, missed the clean air of their land, longed for the gentle touch of their mothers. Then, after a few years, they would buy a fancy suit and return to their villages—not just Nawara, because this was happening all over the country, but I can only tell you the stories I know—and they came back to visit, or marry, or stay.

The problem was that the minute they got here with their eyes that had been trained to see glitter, they criticized their old houses, and they grumbled about the old ways of the village that seemed to come from the time of Muhammad himself, God bless him and grant him salvation. To make a long story short, they couldn't stand it.

Exactly, just like your Uncle Hamdi, who can't sit still after he's been back a week's time, though he is more extreme since he chose an American woman to be his wife. These men were the same way. Unlike my oldest son, your uncle Hamdi, most would compromise and come back to marry and take their brides with them as permanent keepsakes of the village they were leaving behind, if not forever at least for a fair part of their lives.

And just like Hamdi, they got bored after a few weeks home and would go running back to their busy lives.

Karim Sulayman was bored even before he left. He came from an old family who had always been wealthy, tilling that same fertile plot of land and living in the same old house, which thanks to the money he made, we now call a villa, for generations and generations. And surely there are no roses lovelier than the ones Nadia Sulayman grows.

Karim was no smarter than any of the Sulaymans of your generation and never finished high school. We always said they were a family of much business sense but no other sense. At nineteen, he left for America, where a cousin on his mother's side of the family had gone two years earlier.

He came home for the first time a few years later. I remember that day very clearly. I was at the window when I saw a car driving slowly by with lots of people following it—like ants on a piece of raw meat—so I came down and joined the crowd to see who it was. I remember as if it was yesterday, when Karim stopped in front of the house and got out of the car in the finest clothes I have ever seen, as if to announce his prosperity to every one of us poor villagers he had left behind. I am ashamed to say that I, along with most of the village, was very impressed.

Well, it turned out he had come for a bride.

Karim has returned to Nawara almost every year since then, usually with Buthayna and his increasing lot of children in tow. Rumors preceded him about the source of his money, but no one said anything because he always appeared in a whirlwind of generosity. He and his wife carried expensive suitcases filled with the finest of America's goods, bedspreads, deodorants, aspirin, and batteries, and his wallet was stuffed with dollars as fresh and green as the fields he had left. There was always enough to go around too, and it seemed that he was living up to his name.

Then Karim returned again, briefly, with a fat wad of bills with which he intended to endow a mosque. We were ecstatic, less for the mosque itself than for the evidence that once our men went to America, it did not mean that they left forever our humble village of Nawara. It was like proof to the Israelis that we could not be vanquished: we also had American dollars being channeled in to turn our dirt roads to tar and our rubble to mosques.

That spring morning just before dawn, most us were fast asleep, when suddenly *"ALLAHU AKBAR"* tore through the silent air once, and then again *"ALLAHU AKBAR."*

It was indeed the mosque that Karim Sulayman had built, with its grand minaret and four speakers, that had wakened me.

That day, our village was bursting with chatter of the great mosque of Karim Sulayman. Everywhere I went, someone had something to say about it.

"Indeed he is a generous man. And he built the mosque so near the center of the village that we can all reach it without the strain of walking up hills and tripping over rocks. It is a mosque for the old as well as for the young . . . truly a thoughtful man," said one person.

"The minaret he built reaches up toward God. It is as impressive as if it were in one of our large and great cities, like Jerusalem or Cairo," added another, smiling.

"He brought with him the technology of America and gave his minaret four large and powerful speakers to call the faithful from all corners of the village."

"The speakers! But God is wonderful and those speakers are so powerful they carried me to the mosque on the power of their voice alone."

Thus went the talk in the village for the rest of the day. Among the old it took longer to address the actual subject of the speakers, but among the young it was the first thing to cross their lips.

"Can you believe the damn call to prayer this morning?"

"God damn Karim Sulayman and his impressive money. May God curse the speakers made in America and dropped by conspiracy in the village of Nawara."

Nor were the women of Nawara silent, though their cursing was sprinkled with a greater degree of pride for the generosity of Karim Sulayman.

"The voice of this mosque is stronger than the voice of the Knesset itself."

"The morning was a time of peace, now it is a time of American technology. May God forgive my harsh words."

That night silence fell on Nawara earlier than usual and by nine o'clock I was sound asleep.

The next morning, the sun was timidly making its way toward the horizon, perhaps fearful of another blast like the one it had received the previous day.

"ALLAHU AKBAR! ALLAHU AKBAR!"

Suddenly the mosque's call was followed by machine-gun fire.

I don't know why, but I got up, dressed, grabbed my flashlight, and then went out to see what was happening.

What we saw at the base of the minaret was enough to light the gray skies of our souls for many weeks to come. By the time I had arrived, there were many people already there. In the center of the group was a trio of settlers holding machine guns and barking at everyone in a mix of Hebrew, Arabic, and English.

No, I wasn't. Perhaps because it was so early, or perhaps because I suspected they would not fire on the mosque, I was not scared. In fact, no one seemed scared. No one said anything as the three men went on shouting and waving their machine guns in the air.

"It must stop!" shouted the largest of the settlers in heavily accented Arabic. At first I didn't know what he was talking about, but then I realized, along with everyone else, that the mosque's message calling the faithful was too loud for the occupants of the settlement over the hill on the south side of the village.

The *mukhtar*, who is usually very nice, is famous for his need for sleep. He stood in front of this small group of bearded men dressed in blue jeans, with skullcaps pinned to their hair. He said nothing. Not a word. He just stared at them.

No, I don't think he did it out of any principle. I think he was still half asleep and he couldn't think of anything to say.

Eventually the trio of settlers turned and walked through a space that the villagers cleared for them toward another, larger group of settlers who were watching from a few yards off.

After they left, we stood there, sleep still decorating our faces, and watched the settlers drive back to the settlement under the cold morning and the approaching dawn. As they got farther and farther away—I will never forget that moment, my child—as they got farther away, people began to laugh, to themselves at first, but as the dark minutes got brighter—for the sun had not been frightened away after all—the laughter grew and grew until it was like a roar of thunder from beneath the minaret.

"God keep Karim Sulayman and his giant American loud-speakers," cried one man.

"May God be satisfied with him," agreed several others.

Still giggling, we all returned to our houses.

When the sun had showed itself in full, but not long after that, two men set about fixing the giant speakers affixed to the four sides of the minaret. One had to be removed and needed parts, which would take a long time, and one was knocked slightly from its position and had a couple of bullet holes in it, but on the side so it was not seriously damaged. All day long you could find a few people standing beneath the minaret watching and often muttering praises for Karim Sulayman.

And from that day on, Mawal, during those moments before dawn, when the sun is debating whether to greet Nawara, and the giant blast announcing God's greatness crosses the fields of the village, I always mutter a praise for Karim Sulayman.

I tuck this story into my pocket, wishing I could stitch it into my skin, like one of the Bedouin tattoos my grandmother wears. Are there stories like this in lovely, tempting America? Do my cousins there even know these little histories? I doubt it.

Stitch in red for life.

Stitch in green to remember.

Stitch, stitch to never forget.

14

....

BIRTHDAY

We were at Auntie Maysoun's new house in Glendale. She decided to make a party for my birthday. She cooked a lot of food and my cousins danced all night. We don't usually give each other presents, but my American auntie Fay sent me a diary. It's pale green and has a shell on the cover. She wrote my name on the inside with a skinny black pen: KHADIJA MUNEER.

"Why would anyone want a book with blank pages?" Ma asked me.

"So I can write my own book," I told her in English.

Ma doesn't like Auntie Fay.

In the card she sent with the diary, Auntie Fay wrote: "The book is so you can write your secrets and no one will have to know them."

Ma, who doesn't read English, asked me what it said. Instead of saying "secrets," I said "stories and things," but I don't think she believed me. She'll probably have someone else read the card and translate it for her.

Everyone else, including my mother, was outside eating. I came in to bring some more soda and I heard Maysoun telling her sister-in-law, Dahlia, about my mother, her own sister.

"She lets them speak English at home," she hissed. "She treats them like American children. She cooks American food for them. The worst thing she does, though, is she lets them talk back to her. If my Tariq or Soraya did that, they would get a beating, and that would be the last of it. And talk about beatings . . ."

Then Auntie Maysoun went on and on about how Baba hits us too much and then again how Ma gives in to him and to us and is a softie, which will make us very difficult and ultimately disloyal.

Ma says Maysoun is fake and talks big but has nothing inside her. Maysoun smokes and wears gold jewelry and fancy sandals like a young bride. Ma also says Maysoun criticizes others so much because she can't accept that her own daughter is practically a whore.

That's another reason why it's better to be a boy, because then you don't have to spend all your time noticing what everyone does wrong.

15

....

THE AMERICAN DREAM

*O*ur house has an endless supply of visitors, as though this were Nawara.

Saturday, Ma made a party for Khadija's birthday. She knows that if she doesn't, no one else will. It's mostly family and food and dancing and gossips, which sometimes gets on my last nerve and sometimes doesn't.

Today it doesn't, and I help my mother coax a story from her sister-in-law, Dahlia.

"Dahlia, *habibti,* tell us what happened to you," Ma says.

"Maysoun, you can't want to hear that story again. Shame on you. It's over and done with and time to move on."

I pretend I haven't heard it before. "What happened?" I ask.

"*Yulla,* go on. Tell her."

"*Tayeb.* Okay, okay." Dahlia settles into her chair and begins. . . .

It was a spring-air, flower-smell, Los Angeles kind of day— after all these years I remember it clearly. So many details to tell you: like the huge blue sky in the morning and the black sky in the night that can never get dark. It confuses the days and makes them gray, even when the sun is out.

Wait, you also need to know about my life before the incident.

All right, go ahead, Dahlia, tell us everything.

Twenty-seven years old and already a wrinkled and achy mother of four, husband injured at his job in this country with so many rules and benefits that he can stay home accumulating government assistance and watching me out of the corner of his eye, though sometimes I forget which one can see.

"Don't go to work," he tells me so many times. "It's shameful."

But I don't see it that way. What's shameful is an able-bodied man sitting at home on his no-good ass watching his wife clean and cook and do mothering things while he spends all his government assistance money on nothing: a couch with plastic covering and beer that he shouldn't be drinking in the first place.

What's truly shameful is those funny-looking four children holding their bellies and stealing candy bars from 7-Eleven because no one gives them enough of anything to take their aches away.

So one of those lovely spring mornings that smells of familiar flowers, I decide to go to work. It takes a while but it's not too long before I find a job as a nurse's aide at Desert Acres Convalescent Hospital, which means I work ten hours a day wiping drippy asses with skin so loose it's like used-up cheesecloth dripping with rotted fruit. Smells like that too. No one says thank you, only speak louder because they think if you don't speak their language, well, that it also means you don't hear very well and that you're dumb.

"Oh, girl," calls one withered white lady with skin like dough, cold and powdered. "Girl, could you adjust my bed, please."

I get stuck on the word *adjust* for a minute and look at her. Just as it clicks in my head she raises her voice. "Girl, please adjust my bed so I can sit up."

My ears are ringing, but I do what she wants. The convalescent hospital is old, with old walls and old beds and old plumbing, just like the people they've got stored up inside of it.

"Thank you, girl," she says and pats my arm, which surprises me because most of them try to avoid touching you at all, even though you have to touch them in all sorts of places that should make an arm touch not too shameful.

I guess I don't blame them. Their bodies don't work, their minds have wandered off to meet old friends and new horizons, and their own families treat them like they are idiots.

At home such a thing would never happen. At home an old person is revered and cared for. At home most women don't work. Mixed-blessing kind of place, I suppose.

One-mile walk home under spring skies to save bus fare and relax before the zoo that is my other full-time job. Feet like beaten rocks, crumbly and useless, climb up the stairs to find one, two children, half dressed and dirty, and one husband, good for nothing, sleeping passed out on the plastic couch that I hate, more because he insisted we buy it on credit they shouldn't have given us than because it is ugly and uncomfortable.

Better that way. Better no matter how irritating to find him like this. No bothering, no harassment, no when-is-dinner-going-to-be-ready kind of questions.

"Where are your sisters?" I ask Fatima, who laughs her cute little laugh that I have no patience for now.

"My sisters got to go with their uncle for ice cream," she tells me.

"Fatima, please. I'm very tired. Where are your sisters?"

"I told you, Ma, they got to go with their uncle and have ice cream."

"Who is their uncle and where did they go?" I ask, suddenly feeling a pang in my heart.

"Uncle Hector told them Ma was at work and Baba was asleep on the couch and that two could go for ice cream and two had to stay and could go tomorrow."

There is no one in our family named Hector. We have no neighbors I know by that name. In fact, I don't think I have heard the name before, which is how it comes to be that I don't sleep that night and instead go to the police station with my pile-of-shit husband who didn't even want to tell the police in the first place because he is so ashamed of himself for not being able to manage to keep an eye on his very own children. I'll be damned if I leave the fate of those two little girls in the hands of a man who can't even find a job.

I feel as though my insides are being torn out and I refuse to think of anything beside the fact that the police will find our daughters and they will be fine and Hector won't have done anything to them.

Early the next morning, which just feels like an extension of the night, I call the Desert Acres Convalescent Home.

"This is Dahlia. I won't be in today. I have a family emergency."

"You don't come today, then don't bother coming back," Helga screams into my ear in words I would understand in a whisper.

I am tempted not to go because if I didn't have this job in the first place, my two daughters would never have wandered off with Hector—and there are still no leads who he is—and

I would have had time to warn them about the evils of this society.

"You go to work," my husband says. "I will find our babies if it's the last thing I do."

I pray to God he finds Hector and our girls are safe.

My crumbled feet rest on the bus, but crack more when I get there as I wash dirty ass after dirty ass—it's amazing how much waste these shriveled bodies produce—and empty their bedpans and change their sheets and all the while Hector is doing God knows what to my daughters.

Despite the exhaustion and panic and continuous feeling that I will throw up, I see the day for what it is, which is clear and beautiful—how cruel the world can be.

Later Mrs. Julienne asks me to adjust her bed.

Adjust reminds me of yesterday and of coming home dead tired with at least the anticipation of four little children waiting for me with so much excitement and how if there had been no *adjust* they would all still be there—and I burst into tears.

"Are they working you too hard?" she asks me, patting my hand.

Her doughy touch triggers an avalanche. Away with the plastic face for this total stranger, all cracks and withers, who's been in the world three times for my once. I break down.

"What's your name, honey?"

"Dahlia," I manage to squeak out between sobs.

"What a lovely name," she tells me, though a lovely name has done nothing for me so far. "Dahlia, what is the matter?"

Out it spills—in English I didn't know I knew—the rest of the avalanche. My country I may never see again. My injured idiot husband who can't even look after our children well enough to keep them from being picked off the street by crazy

Hector. To come this far only to be poorer than you were when you started poor and then to have your children stolen is more than is worth enduring.

Mrs. Julienne's skin is pale, deep pale, not just the usual dead white. "This is terrible. What are you doing here today?"

"They say they fire me if I don't come."

Without so much as a blink or one question more, Mrs. Julienne rings the emergency button for the nurse who comes in immediately.

"I am appalled. Dahlia has a personal emergency. Her two children have been kidnapped. Either you give her the next few days off as paid leave, or I will move to another hospital, taking all of your credibility with me."

The nurse calls her supervisor, who calls the director, who apologizes, calls a taxi, pays for it, and tells me to take all the time I need.

When I get home there are police cars in front of our building and I feel my heart drop to my cracking toes. They are dead, I tell myself. Don't expect anything good because they are dead.

But they aren't dead. They are playing in the living room with Fatima and Selim.

"Mommy," Lina cries as she sees me, and she and Yasmine fly into my arms.

Turns out Hector thought they were the children of someone else who he had a grudge against. He wasn't going to do anything to them, just wanted to scare their parents. When he found out they weren't who he thought, he panicked.

"I ain't no pervert," he announces on what turns out to be international television. "I took them by mistake and then I brought them back, no harm done. They have lovely manners."

Not very impressive in the brains department; he is held on kidnapping charges.

Our family scene that night is very loving and happy. My lazybones husband says he will look for work, and even if it means that *he* is the one who has to clean drippy-skin asses, he doesn't mind because his children need their mother.

The next day I stay home with my four little children who squirm around me like worms while my husband gets up at 6:00 A.M. to start his hunt. I have my doubts, but three days into this routine he comes back at noon with a smile like the Jordan River on his face and says that 7-Eleven down the block has hired him for the night shift. More than minimum wage, no heavy lifting involved, no bus transfers. We're set.

I go back to the convalescent home and learn that Mrs. Julienne's son is a health inspector so her threats have scare in them. I thank her for her kindness.

"I've been saving that threat for the perfect occasion. Thank you for giving me the opportunity to use it," she tells me, holding my hand.

Helga tells me that my job is there if I want it and even if I want it six months from now. "We saw you on the news," a few of the nurses tell me. "Congratulations that your children are back safely."

This is how we kicked the American nightmare out of our lives and bit off a little of the American dream.

This one's a happy-ending story, for a change. I remember when it happened, and I remember how Ma held my hand extra tight when we went to the mall, or other public places. But just like everything, after a while, the kick in the story goes far enough away that you go back to your normal life.

16

....

SOCIAL STUDIES

*F*inally I have something to write in my diary.

I have a new friend. Her name is Patricia, but she likes to be called Patsy.

I told Ma about her and she keeps saying, "Batzy, Batzy."

She is in my Social Studies class. Sometimes we would say hi to each other, but she seemed snobby. She has thick whitish-blond hair. It's always smooth and fluffy and she is constantly playing with it. Sometimes she lifts it up and when it falls it's like water cascading down her back.

I sit behind her if she takes the front-row seat that I like, and when she plays with her hair, some falls on my desk. Her hairs are so shiny, like plastic, and if you make a double knot, you can tie pencils together with them.

The first time I really talked to her was today. Mr. Napolitano was reviewing for our test on world capitals.

"Jordan, DJ?"

"Amman, Mr. Napolitano."

"Good. Of course, that was an easy one for you."

"Burkina Faso, Pat-a-cake?"

Patricia didn't move and I knew she didn't know the answer because she doesn't even know the European capitals.

"Patricia?"

I leaned forward and whispered, "Ouagadougou."

"Wagdoogoo."

"Very good, Pat-a-cake. I can see you have been studying."

When class was over, Patsy turned around and thanked me. "Do you want to eat together?"

"Sure," I said.

We talked awhile and she's nice. Her eyes are so blue.

Ma got mad because I have had a new school friend for three weeks now and I haven't had her over for dinner.

"You shamed?" she asked me in English, which made me feel pretty bad because it's sort of true. It's not that I'm ashamed, but there are things that an American wouldn't understand, like my mother's language or my father's yelling.

I invited Patsy over for dinner anyway, but I hope Ma cooks American food because I don't think Patsy and her blond hair will like our food too much.

17

....

FANCY-DANCE MAN

Some people can't hide who they are, can't lie and paint a prettier picture, because who they are is smeared on their faces. I can't pretend I'm fourth-generation Italian-American because my hairs are too thick and my eyes dance too much. Losing a country is what makes your eyes dance, is what my uncle Haydar told me once. That works for him because he has lost his country. Even though we come from the same place, and I am from the grandfather who was his father, I have been here too long with a father who wants to be too successful for my country to be lost.

My eyes dance because I am alive, but I don't tell Haydar that . . . or Riad al-Ghareeb, Fancy-Dance man, who struts across the world from one girl to another, pouring stories into their too sweet coffees and drugging them with his too green eyes.

Riad Fancy-Dance wants to be anyone but who he is, like the half-American, half-Italian he creates for the lovely blonde who giggles and crosses and recrosses her legs so often that he puts his hand on her thigh just so she'll stop; and the Greek photographer who loves to take snaps of American beauties, like you, *ya sharmuta,* which means whore in Arabic, not oh beautiful one in Greek like she thinks it does.

They know he's foreign because he leans closer to them than American men do and he looks them square in their blue, green, or purple eyes. He's American enough though that he changes his clothes daily and his breath smells minty, which is all part of a sadness he's fashioned into something that men have contempt for and women eat up in one bite.

Riad, Geros, Gianni, whoever he is today, can drug anyone at least a little bit with his sadness that he fashions into exotic characters. And though he grew up in the refugee camps in Lebanon, his body is beefy and strong like an American's. Even when he first came here it was like that. I remember. He always scared me a little, always seemed to be looking behind me when he spoke, maybe searching for ghosts. He worked for my father for a while, but my father had to let him go because he never showed up when he was supposed to.

He lives near us, though, and almost every day I see Riad Fancy-Dance with a new lady lovely he will call *sharmuta* if he's angry or *habibti,* my love, if he's happy. Either way they always think he's wonderful for a day, or a week, or sometimes two.

Not me, though. No matter how handsome Riad Fancy-Dance may be, I know there is something missing in him, and I've seen his eyes when they are red from hashish. He lost his country more than any of us, but what I see ain't dancing; it's searching, like looking for his own self and not being able to find a mirror.

So I know what I'm in for when I see him at the mall and he asks me to have pizza with him, "as a sister, the greatest sister. God always keep you pure."

It's also why I know not to yell when Riad Fancy-Dance ambushes me a different day at the mall, when I am outside smoking away from anyone's view. Along he comes with his green eyes, sad for today, and pleads for my love. I turn away from him and I don't scream at first when he comes from behind and his body parts are touching me. But soon too much of him is on me and all I can do is explode, "God damn you. God damn your lies and your whores. How dare you call me your sister, with all of your lies and your pimp ways . . . !"

He hangs his head and tries to hold on to my hand, to grab any affection I will give him, which is none.

And the next day, which is the last day I ever see him, he asks me to marry him *bi-halal,* which is the opposite of *bi-haram,* in sin. And I tell him he's crazy and no way and get out of here.

Riad Fancy-Dance walks away to pour more drugged stories into the sweetened coffees of lovely American beauties who will hand him their jewels and their innocence in a plastic box and never realize that he has taken them only to try to fill his own empty self.

And I turn to steel the soft part inside of me that wants to crumble with rage and sadness. I'm so sick of everything being *haram* or *halal,* but nothing in between. *I* am in between.

So I drive home with the windows down and the stereo blasting, and even though I can't close my eyes, in my mind I am dancing the rage away.

HALA

18

....

SHARIF

"As-salaamu alaykum."

I am startled by the deep voice that is louder than the television.

"Who is that?" I ask Latifa.

"Probably Sharif," my sister answers, getting up to see. "He has been away on business for a couple of weeks."

"Who?"

"Don't you remember? He is our cousin, Hala. He went to Europe for several years and just came back last year. Now he and our father enjoy each other's company and Baba treats him like his own son."

I go through the pictures of our Jordanian relatives I have stored up in my mind, but I cannot remember.

"Sharif. Sharif Abdel-Hameed."

Sharif Abdel-Hameed from our mother's side. I remember Sharif. He was nice to me when I was young. He'd play with me and tease me and bring me candies and pencils. Sometimes he would come and sit with me and talk to me like an adult, asking all sorts of questions. What do you see when you climb the mulberry tree? What makes the rain come down? What is your favorite book? Do you think about home? I never felt shy with him and he was always patient to hear my answers. Then, when I was eight or nine, he went to Europe.

Sharif, like many relatives, drifted in and out of my world. There was a time when he was over all the time, so close to us that he went on vacations with us. His mother is from Nawara and is a cousin to my mother.

Heavy feet approach; Latifa is still standing. She looks ridiculous, like a little girl waiting for her father. It occurs to me that she is in love with Sharif.

"*As-salaamu alaykum,*" Sharif says again when he comes around the corner. "May God protect the rest of the people in this house," he says because my grandmother's memory is still close.

"Welcome, Sharif," my sister says with an especially large smile. "Thank God for your safe return. You remember my little sister Hala?"

"Hala, Hala, Hala, and welcome to you, Miss Hala." He looks at me, his brown eyes intense, yet cheerful. It is strange to see him after so long. He has aged more than my brother has, or perhaps just looks that way because he is heavyset, or because of all the hair he has lost. It's not just that, though. Jalal, at twenty-eight, looks as if he's in his prime. Sharif, who is a few years older, looks as if he has been sitting in middle age for a while. He is neat, his solid body tidily packaged in creaseless clothing. We shake hands and his grip is tight, his hand lingers just a moment.

"Hala, little Hala, is now a lovely grown-up Hala." I feel a wave inside of me, as though a giant change is about to occur. My sister has gotten up to make coffee. The two of us are alone.

He sits down and sighs. "Ali, a Lebanese poet I know, says: '*When I was young I loved a woman who never existed*

/ *When I grew up I remembered the woman I loved when I was young.*'" I stare at his hands that are thick like shovels and wonder at his words.

"I have a punching bag at home," he says, as if reading my thoughts and I feel my face burn. "I recite poetry as I punch. It gets out all the unused anger and love that I have stored in me."

He stops for a moment and smiles at my brother's image on the TV screen. Then he turns back to me. "So Miss Hala, American Hala, tell me about your life." He smiles, clear and honest.

I tell him about graduation, about Aunt Fay and Uncle Hamdi, about my university plans, and he listens with the same interest and patience as he did when I was a child, which always made me feel the delight and power of my words.

When Latifa comes back and lowers the tray for him, she leans over so much that her bra shows. I feel embarrassed for her as Sharif looks back at the television screen.

"So you are married and have children now?" I ask him to irritate Latifa.

"No, I am not married and I have no children."

"You are a nosy girl," Latifa says to me as though I were five years old again.

"No, she is as curious as she was when she was a child." He winks at me.

I don't remember him being this charming, and I am amazed at how familiar and comfortable I feel talking to him.

"You are really very lucky you came home when you did," Sharif tells me when Latifa has left the room. "I have some free time and, as luck would have it, I am a professional tour guide. I would be delighted to reacquaint you with your homeland. One of your homelands, at least."

"That would be great."

"What would be great?" asks Latifa, who has reappeared.

"I was telling Hala what a grand tour guide I am. As I have the liberty of a summer free of work or worries, I will dedicate it to the two of you and your desires. We will see the castles; we will eat in all the new restaurants; we will have picnics. We will *not* go to Aqaba, may God have mercy on your mother. You will be so tired of me after these few weeks that you, Miss Hala, will run back to America in exhaustion."

I laugh. Latifa does not.

"That would be very nice, Sharif, but please do not trouble yourself on our behalf. I can take Hala wherever she needs to go."

"My dear sister, Latifa, need is not the issue. I am speaking of desire and wishing. She may *need* to go to the store to buy shampoo, but she may *desire* to go to Ata Ali for ice cream. And that, my friends, is a splendid idea. Let us have some ice cream."

Latifa has started to make noises of protest, but Sharif ignores her.

"This is really the best time for ice cream, you know. You see, it is long enough after breakfast that you are hungry, but too early for lunch. This way, you will eat your lunch later, meaning your belly will be full later in the day, so you will have a light dinner and then sleep with enough food for good dreams and a content stomach that won't even contemplate indigestion."

I giggle and get up.

"Ice cream it is."

And after ice cream it is driving through the new neighborhoods to look at houses that have been built on what were fields when I was last here. And more driving with loud music. And more driving and lunch. By the time we get home, I am full and exhausted. Later, when I am going to sleep, I cannot shake Sharif's face from my mind.

19

....

LOOKING

Sometimes stories in our house come from watching, watching just the right way and seeing the underside of things, the thinking things and the forgetting things.

"Watch your grandmother," my mother has always told me, especially when my grandmother was strong and her eyes were still lively. "She is getting older, may God give her strength. Watch what she can tell you."

And so I watch my grandmother.

Sun hits aged, fading white walls like stale bread. One old woman, her head wrapped in colors, stands in front of her unshuttered window to look. She surveys the hills and the orange trees under which her six children played before they grew and left, but she does not think about them as she looks out and sees a land as beautiful as it was before.

A shepherd leads his goats to the far corner of her land and she sees this, her wrapped head shaking back and forth as it does every time the gnarled man stops to let his goats graze on the tasty grasses.

There is quiet life in the air: crackles and wind noises and bird songs. She rests her arms on the sill and watches, her eyes scanning the slope to the valley where her husband was killed, and though her son Haydar was a witness to the murder, she does not think about this now.

The woman with creases in her face, deep like the sand beneath the desert, rests here, though laziness is not her nature and the old house is usually filled with the clap clap clap of her slippers against concrete that is so cold in winter it seems like outside.

The joyous scarf suggests that the hair beneath it is lustrous and wild, and while once it was considered to be the most beautiful hair in the village, for some reason it began to fall out on her wedding night, and has left hennaed tufts and gaps in its place.

She fills her eyes with the whiteness of her neighbor's wall, and in that direction the blueness of the sky, and over there the greenness of the treetops. As she looks, she wonders at God's creation and beauty and longs to stretch out like water on the ground underneath the sun, knowing that no one will see. But her elbows remain on the sill, eyes fixed on white then blue then green.

Looking toward the small hut where the chickens live, she smiles, for she will always see her daughter Shahira's baby Mina on her hands and knees as though she too were a chicken with her nose going back and forth from ground to sky.

She does not think of Mina and her sad departure to the States with her sister, mother, and stepfather, because she has taught herself to look above the treetops and into the colors.

20

....

AQABA

At night after we have eaten, and visited, and talked, I listen to music and remember. My mother loved the Lebanese singer Fairuz. She said that she never heard a voice that carried a person's soul as much as hers.

Tonight I remember Sharif and the summer when I was five or six that my father took us all to Aqaba. Sharif, who was nineteen or twenty, came with us.

Everyone else is playing at the other end of the beach except Sharif, who is teaching me how to dive cleanly into the water. My ears shut to his words sometimes because the water is so clear that if I stand still and look down I can see my feet.

The sky is light blue and the water where it meets the sky is dark blue.

"Can we swim out there to where the two blues meet?" It doesn't look so far and I think Sharif will like my idea.

He looks out to the sea and doesn't say anything. Shading his eyes with his hand, he turns his head from left to right.

I see a small shell under the water but when I go to grab it, the water moves and it vanishes.

"Let's swim home," he says with his face still in the sun.

"Home? This beach won't reach to Amman. How can we swim there if there is no water?" I try to stay still so my shell will come back.

"I mean to Palestine." He turns to look at me.

"We can't swim to Palestine."

"Why not? She's right there." He points to the right, below the sun. We are so close that I can see the houses on the shore.

"That's Palestine?"

He nods, still looking.

I feel funny inside. "We're not allowed to go there. It's not our home anymore." The water is very blurry now.

"Says who?" He stares at me with his hands in fists at his waist.

I feel scared. My cousin seems very big. I look back down to see the pretty shell under the water, but all I see is swirling.

"Hey! We can take those!" He points to the hotel next to ours. In front are orange, green, blue, and yellow dolphins pulled up on the hot sand. "Paddleboats. Come on, little girl, let's go."

Sharif pushes our dolphin away from the beach. We pedal slowly because I cannot move my legs as fast as he can. In front of us are two huge cargo ships, behind us is the beach, and to the right is Palestine. I think that Saudi Arabia is behind the ships.

I stop pedaling and look over the side. The water is deep but I can see the bottom clearly and there is a green and white soda can lying on the sand beneath. We pedal more and I feel very small. "Can we go look at those ships? Maybe they have treasures."

"No, those are commercial ships."

"What's on them?"

"There could be anything. Like cars or canned food or refrigerators or even frozen Australian meat."

The ships look huge and I want to be back in the water where I can stand up and see my toes.

"I suppose we could see what that beach over there is like." He is looking to the left.

It looks the same as our beach but with more trees and no hotels. "Okay." I am tired of pedaling.

"Why did the Hebronite leave the door to the bathroom open?" he asks.

"I don't know," I say, even though my brother has told this joke a hundred times.

"So no one would watch him through the keyhole." He slaps his leg and throws back his head, like this is the funniest thing he ever heard. I feel happy to be in the middle of the sea with this big cousin of mine and his silly jokes.

He stops pedaling. "You know, little Hala, that coast looks the same except that there are more trees and the sand is whiter."

"We could go to Saudi Arabia."

"Too hot. Too conservative."

"Let's go in the other direction so our faces get warm," I say. We turn around.

A motorboat zooms by and makes a big wave and I get scared because I think our orange dolphin will turn over. Just when the sea becomes like a sheet, another motorboat tries to scare the dolphin, only this one has guns and two soldiers. We don't move until their wave is gone and the dolphin has stopped tipping from side to side. I want to cry, but I look at Sharif. He is sitting up very straight, as if he is challenging the sun.

He squints. "Do you still want to go home?"

At first I think he means Amman again and I am confused,

but I see him looking at the other shore and I understand. I turn around in my seat. The boat with the soldiers is stopped a small distance away and one of them is watching us. I start to wave but Sharif stops me.

Sharif pedals and now we move faster. He sings a song from home that my mother sometimes sings. I listen and watch the houses. I can see plants on the window ledges. The beach behind us looks very far away, but I feel safe. We pedal and sing and challenge the sun.

I hear a motor and then a wave comes from a different direction this time. I turn and see the soldiers coming straight at us.

"Sharif, let's ask them for a ride in their boat."

He doesn't hear me, just keeps pedaling.

The soldier boat turns off its motor in front of us and our dolphin rocks in its wave.

"Hello!" one of them calls.

Sharif stops pedaling but is still staring at the houses.

I feel scared, but I want to ride on their boat.

"Where are you going?" Their boat has floated up to ours and they are both young—maybe even younger than Sharif—and look smaller than they looked from a distance.

"Home," I answer because Sharif is silent.

"Home?" The soldier has big teeth.

I feel shy and look down.

"We just wanted to see what's on that shore." Sharif points to the houses.

"You can't go there." The soldiers laugh. "They won't let you."

"Who is 'they'?" I ask. Sharif is quiet.

"The Israelis. You can't cross this border"—he points a few feet in front of us—"or they will come out and stop you. They might even hurt you."

I look at the houses.

"You're awfully far from the beach. Why don't we take you back." The soldier has a nice voice, but I don't want to go with them anymore.

Sharif turns to me with large eyes. He tickles me. "Come on."

The soldier with the big teeth pulls our boats side by side and helps me get up and into their boat. Sharif gets in by himself. They tie the string from the dolphin to their boat and we turn back toward our shore. I wish they would go faster.

The soldiers are asking where we are from and I answer, but Sharif is leaning over the side, letting the water splash his face and watching the houses.

We reach the shore and I see a small cluster of people waiting for us. Latifa is standing next to my father and both of them have their hands on their hips. Even from this distance I can see that she is happy, perhaps excited that I am about to get into trouble. My mother is standing at the shoreline, the waves covering her feet and some of her dress. She is wringing her hands and yelling, but we are still too far away to hear what she is saying.

Before the soldiers even pull the dolphin up on the beach, my mother is in the water with her shouts for me and for Sharif. My father has walked away and left Latifa to watch. My mother grabs me and kisses me with so much strength and anger that I think she would rather hit me. "Thank God you are safe. Thank God you are alive," she says in my ear over and over.

She puts me down and turns to Sharif with the loudest, angriest voice I have ever heard her use. "What in God's name are you doing with such a baby in such deep waters? She cannot swim. She could have drowned. You are a man and this is the kind of thing you do to your baby cousin!" It goes on and on and I don't even notice when the soldiers leave. Sharif hangs his head, except when my mother yanks at his ear or slaps his arm.

"Where did you think you were going? Why did you just go off into the middle of the sea like that without telling anyone?"

Sharif doesn't look at anything but his feet. I can't understand why he doesn't speak, why he doesn't explain.

My mother is still yelling and other people on the beach are watching us. Finally, I can't stand her words and his silence. "We tried to go home!" I shout.

They both stare at me. My mother is silent and then starts scolding Sharif again, but I see it is softer and she is no longer yanking at his ear or slapping him. We walk up the beach and she picks me up and hugs me, gently this time, and even though she is still cursing him, I know that all of the anger has washed out of her.

That is the sweet picture in my mind as I drift off to sleep, surrounded by my mother's presence.

21

....

VISITING

*E*arly the next morning as I lie in bed listening to the morning sounds, I hear a car and then Sharif's voice calling, "*Assalaamu alaykum*" and I feel my heart speed up. I go to the window and see him, sitting with my father on the chairs that face the white wall. I force myself to take my time getting out of bed, trying to ignore the sweaty nervousness that is creeping underneath my skin.

When I finally go to the main part of the house, Latifa is nowhere in sight and Sharif and my father are still sitting in the chairs with a coffeepot on the table between them.

"Good morning," I say from the doorway.

Sharif stands up and bows. "And the best of good mornings to you. I hope that you have awakened from a most delightful sleep."

What do I say to someone who talks this way?

"I have informed your father of my tour guide abilities and he has given his approval. The tour will begin today, late morning, for a visit to my mother. Latifa has already been informed and is making the necessary preparations. I am hoping this meets with your approval."

 "Indeed it does," I say and giggle.

"Europe has given Sharif more words than he knows what to do with. Maybe we should call him 'The Orator Without an Audience.'"

"All due respect, Abu Jalal, but I believe I have an audience of a most attentive nature."

My father smiles. "I must get on with the day." He gets up and brushes by me without another word.

"I have to do a couple of errands and then I will be back for the two of you," Sharif says and winks.

I always liked Sharif's mother. She never made me feel that she was judging me and, like her son, always seemed interested in whatever I had to say. She was so happy for me when I told her I was going to the States.

Even though I saw her when I first arrived for an official greeting, this time is warmer with plenty of hugs and kisses and more hugs and squeezes. She is looking old, but she is still very strong. She sits us all down and goes to make coffee. Latifa gets up to help her, as she does anywhere we go, and Um Sharif stops her.

"Please, Latifa, do not come to my house and work. You deserve a little peace." Latifa is clearly pleased and sits back in the chair smiling.

When Um Sharif comes back she starts asking me questions, just the way her son does. "Do you like living away from home? Is it very different there for you? Is your uncle Hamdi very American? Are you going to stay longer?" The questions seem endless.

When I finish my coffee, she takes my cup to read the grounds. Holding the cup in front of her, she turns it around and around in her hand. "You have just come from a very long trip for the sake of others, but soon it will be your turn. There is a lion knocking on your door." She winks when she says this part and Sharif laughs.

"What does that mean? Is it bad?" I ask, but she turns to Latifa and asks her questions that won't let me get my question in.

Later, when we are back in the car I ask Sharif what his mother meant. It's Latifa who answers. "It means that a man is about to ask you to marry him or to fall in love with you."

I feel my face turn red and I turn toward the window as I imagine my father bargaining to get rid of his youngest daughter.

Sharif stops at a store and buys cigarettes and Pepsi. He then heads out of the city toward Ajlun. The driving is so peaceful. I'm in the backseat of his black Fiat with the windows down, and Muhammad Munir's Egyptian voice so loud I can't hear anything Sharif and Latifa are saying, which is fine. I watch the hills and trees and villages, imagining the people who live there, wondering if my mother thought of her village every time she drove by Jordanian villages. Being away has made me see the country as more beautiful. I am even enjoying Latifa. Away from the house she seems relaxed, like a different person. She and Sharif seem to be comfortable with each other.

"Ladies and gentlemen, if you look just ahead of you, you will get your first glimpse of the castle and you will notice along the side of the road there is a watermelon stand." Just as he says this, he turns the car off the road, stops, and gets out. When he returns, he is carrying a huge watermelon. We drive slowly the rest of the way to the castle. We find a shady spot to park and sit under a tree eating sticky, cool, delicious watermelon. (Prepared as always, Sharif keeps a "water-melon knife" in his glove compartment.)

"I lived in Rome for some time," Sharif begins. "I had an Italian friend who gave tours. One day he was supposed to give a tour to a group of Americans, but got very sick and implored me to take his place. I thought this would be no problem. One of the first things I did in Rome was the historical tour—I thought I knew everything there was to know. Alas, I was wrong. I knew the major sights, of course, but you would be amazed at how many *piazze* and *fontane* these people wanted to know about. I had no choice but to use my imagination. I kept trying to think of the names of famous Italians, but I ran out quickly. The historical section of my brain only does our history. I stood at the microphone pointing right and left: 'Here is Piazza dei Nasseri. Over there is Via Santo Antaro. Wait until you see Castello degli Angeli Che Amano i Palestini.' Fortunately, they were young Americans and no one seemed to notice."

So funny to think of those historical, literary, and political words translated for fun, the last one especially, which Sharif says means "Castle of the Angels Who Love the Palestinians."

He goes on and on about Italy and France and Greece and we listen. He tells jokes that are as silly as they were fifteen years ago, but Latifa and I laugh anyway. When we finish eating, we walk through the castle.

"This way, this way," Sharif says as we pass tourists. Up and up and up and we reach the highest part of the castle, which looks out over a small valley. We sit there silently for what seems like a very long time, legs dangling over the edge and a story here and there to fill our ears. It is like sitting with the oldest friends in the world, no words are necessary, but when they come, they are most welcome. For the first time since I have been back, I feel at peace.

With this day, a new chapter in my life begins, a new beginning after my grandmother's death. Sharif comes over every day to take us somewhere: to the *souq*, the mall, visiting
friends or relatives, to Jerash, to Ajlun, wherever our hearts
desire. Latifa likes Jerash. Ajlun is my favorite. This is the
perfect way to come home and taste it all over again. Even
though I feel I don't know enough about him, Sharif makes
me laugh, often uncontrollably, like the time when we were
at a stoplight in Amman—I was in the front seat for once—
and a boy on the median was selling gum. He leaned very
close to the car and said, "Gum for your daughter?" Sharif
looked at me, then looked back at the boy and said, "No
thank you. It would be torture for her. You see, she doesn't
have any teeth.".

Each morning I take my time getting dressed, something I
never paid much attention to before. I have become self-
conscious, not in a pretty/ugly way, just aware of myself and
my body. I notice everything, and not just in me. Colors are
sharper. All sensations are exaggerated. Food is delicious or
vile. Sights are magnificent or hideous. Smells are divine or
nauseating. I cannot explain what is happening to me. Sharif
is like my brother and is making me see my country in a way
I never have. I am beginning to think he is in love with
Latifa—though surely this is not possible. I look forward to
our outings together more than to anything else. My disappointment is enormous if for some reason he cannot come.
And then there is this extra heart-beating feeling, which I cannot even begin to explain.

One day we drop Latifa off to get her hair done.
　　"I live close by," Sharif says.
　　My thoughts are elsewhere. "You know, Latifa likes you."

"I know," he says. "Her spirit is very heavy."

"So you don't like her that way?"

"There is only one sister of my dear friend and cousin Jalal whom I consider to be a princess."

My heart is in my mouth and we drive in silence.

"I want to see where you live," I say, though the minute the words are out of my mouth I am ashamed and I want to take them back.

Without hesitation, he turns the car around and goes back toward where we left Latifa.

The windows are down and dry wind whips my hair across my face and in my eyes, but I lean my head out farther. Stillness in the air, louder than the car engine.

My mouth is so dry I am almost gasping. We pull up in front of a store and Sharif buys two Pepsis and a cluster of small bananas. We drive, twisting and turning. He puts a whole banana in his mouth and throws the peel out the window.

Sweat is everywhere, on his forehead and dripping down by his ears. Wet marks form under his arms and I can feel the sweat under my jeans.

We turn down a narrow road lined with box houses. He stops in front of one of them. "Welcome," he says.

Two rooms. In the corner of the living room hangs a punching bag, dark and green and somber and I imagine the corpses of poems scattered under it. Dotting the base of the walls are small coffee cups with thick grounds caked at the bottom. A radio stands sentry in the corner. Three small chairs cluster against the far wall, as though the last occupants were huddled together in conference.

Hot thick air, no breeze, no movement. I know I shouldn't be here.

"Welcome," he says again.

I feel shy, as though I have entered a house uninvited. I walk to the punching bag and hit it, just to see how hard it is.

"Here," he says, taking my hand. "Fold your fist like this. Thumb down and under so it won't get broken. Good. Punch comes from the side. Half twist around. Finger tips go from looking at the sky to looking at the floor."

I watch his arms, thick like branches. I hear the *thunk* his fist makes when it meets the bag.

"Go ahead. You try."

I do as he says. He guides my arm, my fist, and soon it is making the same thunks that his did.

"Clever girl."

My arm aches. We stand and look at each other in silence for a minute.

"We must go," he says, and I feel again as though I should not have come. We drive back to the hair salon and wait for Latifa outside.

That night I cannot sleep. Sharif is with me more and more. I feel a smothering feeling; I am losing control. Of what? I am not in love with him. I need to get away.

22

....

THE BEAUTIFUL GIFT

Sitti, my mother's mother, is dying. It will be soon, before the summer ends; that's what everyone says. Auntie Shahira is going to come. Maysoun can't leave the store. Haydar is crazy. Huda is dead. My mother is here. That leaves Hamdi, the oldest son. But he is too busy with his American life, with his American wife, to come say good-bye. Or even hello.

He calls every once in a while. He sends money. He's not that different from Um Radwan's children, because he really wants to forget. . . . Which reminds me of when Hamdi did come to visit so many years ago.

Like yesterday, like tomorrow. It was early summer, still cool in the morning, with a clean crispness, like new sheets for a wedding. A week before they came, my mother and grand-mother began scrubbing Sitti's house from top to bottom, front to back, side to side (should we do it left to right or right to left?). Scrubbing, then rinsing, then scrubbing again. My father oiled old doors. My mother did laundry and scrubbed some more. My father painted and adjusted the antenna on the roof.

"God willing, my oldest son will come every year," Sitti said with a wink, admiring her clean old house scrubbed like new.

"What do you think they will bring us?" I asked my mother the day before they came, though this idea had been in my head for days.

"Shame on you. Perhaps they will bring you one sour American lemon."

"*Yama!* What do you think they really will bring?" My mother clicked her tongue and ignored me. The thoughts stayed there in my head. Big fat thoughts . . . a beautiful plastic doll with long legs and long yellow hair, a fancy dress I could wear to weddings, a fancy American toy that did tricks—it didn't really matter. I was sure it would be wonderful. Then I could have something to show off to Hanan, God forgive me my greedy thoughts.

Hanan lived down the road from us in a fancy villa. She was born in the States, and came back when she was four. She had her own room with huge furniture and fancy plastic toys. My mother said she was spoiled, but not in a good way, like the kind who has too many things (*The more you give them, the more they want*) and wants so much more to fill some empty spot we can't see. She was the only person I knew who had that many toys.

She also saw things. Not things like ghosts and *jinn*, but magical things in the ordinary everyday things, like a crumpled wrapper lying in the street.

"Look," she'd say. "It's a poor old man on his knees begging for mercy from his wife who he's cheated on."

I would stare at it.

I would stare harder.

And I would see a crumpled wrapper.

Later I'd catch her looking up.

I'd look to where she was looking.

"A giant horse is carrying away two orphan children, but one has fallen in the river and the horse can't turn around to pick it up."

I would stare at the clouds. I would look exactly where she was looking. I would stand so close to her that her soft brown hair tickled my ear, but all I could see was a cloud, that—if I crossed my eyes a little—could look like a boat.

"Why does she see those things?" I asked my mother.

"Same thing that got her father rich while the rest of the people just get by," she said. "Maybe they eat magic lentils."

"Why don't you try to cook us some magic lentils?" I asked her, only half joking.

"Only some people can have visions. Others will be happy."

"How could someone who can't see those beautiful visions be happier than someone who can?" I asked, but she clicked her tongue and looked away.

That day before Uncle Hamdi was supposed to come, I told Hanan.

"They're coming from America?"

"Yes. They are both professors in a university. She is American and doesn't speak Arabic. My mother is very happy they are coming and is cooking lots of delicious food." I hoped Hanan was impressed, especially by the American wife.

"Mmm." Hanan was quiet for a minute. "I won't see you for a few days. We're going to Nablus. My mother's sister just had an operation and we're going to go help out."

Disappointment like a slap. The one time I had something to show off and not only was she not going to be around to see it, but she was going all the way to Nablus. Like she was trying to top my relative-visiting story with her own visiting-relative story.

We said good-bye, and when I went inside I found my

mother and grandmother in the kitchen rolling grape leaves. I have never had stuffed grape leaves except during Ramadan.

"Yum! All of this for my uncle?" I asked.

My mother looked happy. "No, all of this for you and your sunshine smile." She kissed me on the forehead. "Go wash your hands and come help us."

The next day we got up early and went to Sitti's house to clean some more and to cook. Bajis left with his yellow license plates and my father to go to the airport in Tel Aviv. Neighbors and relatives drifted in and out all day.

I swept and played and dusted and played, and then I went out on the balcony to wait. Finally, I saw the small white van tottering up the road. "They're here, they're here!" I yelled.

Sitti and my mother ululated as the van pulled in front of the house. After a moment Hamdi and Fay unfolded their tall selves out, followed by kisses and tears and cousins and neighbors and shouts.

Hamdi came over and lifted me up for kisses. I didn't know him except from pictures, but he was so familiar, maybe because he wears a little of my mother's face on his. He was very tall, taller than my father, and his wife, Fay, was almost as tall as he is. I had never met an American before, and I felt shy in front of her smooth, white face. She had kind eyes, though, and when she came over and gave me kisses on both cheeks, followed by a big, squeezing hug, I could see that she was nervous too. My mother was greeting Fay and I held her hand as we walked up to the house.

This day was so nice, filled with food and stories and shyness and English. Fay sat next to me when she could, and Hamdi kept telling my mother that I looked just like her. It was strange having our house filled with a language I didn't understand.

I had forgotten about the present I was waiting for, when

Uncle Hamdi called to me from downstairs. "Mawal, come help me with something."

I ran down the stairs, and there at the bottom was a beautiful red bicycle with white handlebars and a giant pink bow on the white seat.

"Is that for me!"

My uncle, my father, Fay, and Sitti were all smiling at me.

"Look at me," my mother said from behind me. When I turned around a flash of light went off.

"A camera?" I asked.

"This is *my* present from Uncle Hamdi and Auntie Fay," she said, smiling.

I kissed my uncle and Fay and thanked them. Then I went to the bike and sat on the seat. My feet reached the ground. It seemed as though it had been made for me. I couldn't believe they had brought me this beautiful bicycle. I don't think there was a single girl in the whole village who had a bicycle, a real, metal bicycle.

"You will probably learn how to ride it in a day or two because you're such a smart girl," Uncle Hamdi told me.

We stood at the head of the driveway that leads to Sitti's house.

"You climb on and I will hold the back until you get your balance," my uncle said.

I did as I was told. Pedaled, pedaled slowly with my uncle walking behind me, holding tight, and my mother click click clicking her lovely new Minolta instant focus camera.

I couldn't believe this. I felt so happy. Everyone, even Sitti, took turns holding the back of the seat for me—and for the other kids—and running as we picked up speed.

It took me less than a week to learn how to ride it without falling. Someone always stayed with me to make sure I didn't go into the main paved street at the end of the dirt road that led up to our house. I learned to give rides to the other kids as well.

On one of those days, Hanan came by with her mother while we were all taking turns riding. "Hi, Hanan, how was—" but before I could ask her about her week in the city, she pointed to the bicycle.

"Whose is that?"

"Mine," I told her proudly.

"Where did you get it?"

"My uncle Hamdi and auntie Fay brought it from America. I already know how to ride it. Watch me."

I stepped up on the bike and began to ride down the drive. I stopped to look back. Hanan was smiling and I felt I could fly as I rode back to her.

"Here, you can try it," I told her.

"I don't know how," she said.

"I'll help you. It's really easy."

Hanan took the handlebars and stood for a moment, as if she was studying it and trying to figure out what to do.

"Like this," I told her and showed her how to get on. "I'll hold the back for you. All you have to do is pedal."

She got on the seat and I held it steady. She put her feet on the pedals and I held the back as she moved forward. "Help!" she cried as she fell, but I caught her before she was all the way on the ground.

"It's okay," I told her as I helped her up. "You will fall a couple of times. That's the only way to learn."

We tried it again, but the same thing happened and she still wasn't sitting straight in the seat. "Why don't we wait until my uncle gets back or my mother comes down to help."

"No, let's try again."

We kept trying, but she couldn't get any speed and would fall over because I couldn't hold the bike steady. We had to stop because my mother called me to come in.

The next day I found my mother alone in the sitting room embroidering.

"Where are Uncle Hamdi and Auntie Fay?" I asked her.

"They are at your grandmother's." She smiled at me and put her embroidery aside. I lay down with my head in her lap. I love the feeling of my mother's fingers wandering through my hair.

"What's this cloud hovering over Little Miss Sunshine?" She poked my nose, my forehead, my chin, and my belly.

"Nothing," I said, though I felt strange inside, like something bad was going to happen.

"Are you sure? It's not good to keep your problems in your belly, because then they grow and grow until you are so fat you look like an elephant and you will have to sleep outside because you won't fit in the door."

I was laughing now and she tickled me.

"Go on. Go ride your new American bike."

I did as I was told and went downstairs with my bike, and she came with me.

"Let's see you ride to the end of the drive, but turn around before you get to the street."

I got on my bike and rode feeling free and happy again. When I got to the end and turned around, I could see my mother smiling.

"Go on, let's see that again. You ride very well," she said when I came back. Again I went to the end of the drive, and this time when I was coming back, I saw both my mother and Hanan watching me. I felt more of that bad feeling, and I don't know why, but I wished that Hanan would go away. This was the first time I had ever thought such a bad thought, and I got dizzy from it, as if my bicycle had replaced her magic and made it seem dirty.

"Hi!" she called as I got closer.

My mother stood up. "You two have fun. Just don't ride down too far."

I felt a bad tingling as I watched her go inside.

"Can I ride your bike?" Hanan asked.

"We should probably wait until my mother comes back to help you. I'm not strong enough to hold the bike up."

"I think it's because the road is bumpy. I'm sure if we rode on the street I would have no problem," she said, smiling.

"I'm not allowed to ride in the street."

"There are hardly any cars. Besides, the street is wide enough in this area to fit a car going in each direction."

"There may not be a lot of cars, but when they come by, they are going very quickly and they are not prepared to stop for someone on a bicycle," I said, repeating my father's words.

"Your beautiful bike deserves to go on the street."

"What do you mean?"

"Your bike is from America and there the streets are all smooth like glass, not rocky like this dirt road."

"But it's doing fine. You saw me riding it."

"Yes, but it might feel sad and want to go on a smooth street."

"The bike?"

"Of course. It might just decide to go on its own to a place that has a nicer surface."

"My mother says—"

"Adults don't understand these things. Only kids like us can understand bikes. Look how sad he looks," she said, pointing to the handlebars. "He's very sad and thinking how he'd like to ride on the street for a little while."

I looked at my lovely red bicycle. I didn't see any sadness or pleading, but Hanan always saw things better than I did anyway. What if she was right? Besides, it's true what she said about there not being a lot of cars on the road. "Well, maybe . . ." I started to say.

"Let's go to the street, just to see if it seems happier."

I got on the bike and rode slowly down the narrow drive while she ran next to me and then behind me as I rode faster. When I got to the end I turned around and waited. The street to either side of me seemed like an ocean, but it was smooth and only two cars went by. When Hanan reached me, she was out of breath.

"Okay, let me try it again." She took the bike from me and tried to get on how I had showed her, pushing off with one foot. She tried three times, and each time caught herself before she fell.

"Why don't we ride on it together," she said.

I held the bike steady for her as she got on and I stood in front of her with the bike between my legs. Looking at the street I felt very tiny, as if I was about to be swallowed, but I started pedaling anyway. At first I could barely make the pedals turn and I thought we would fall, but as I got my balance it was easier. The road went evenly for a while before it sloped down and got easier to pedal.

"This is wonderful," Hanan said, laughing.

It was as though we had entered a whole new world, where the street was a smooth and vast desert. Hanan must have been right that the bike liked it better, and I felt glad that I was giving it what it wanted. I felt as though we were flying as Hanan laughed and held on to me.

We went fast along the street, and suddenly the road was going downhill. I stayed as close to the edge as I could without getting too close to the grass and rocks. I wanted to sit down, but Hanan took the whole seat, so I continued standing up, not even pedaling now. I saw a car coming from down the hill and I thought I heard a car behind us too. I panicked and pulled my feet back quickly to brake. In a blink, I flew over the handlebars into the grass and rocks and weeds just as the car passed—there was only one—and when I looked up Hanan was lying in a pile with the bike on top of her. There was blood on her face, and just as I looked at her she started to cry. I got up and went over to pull the bike off Hanan and my bottom ached from where I landed, but I didn't hurt besides there. Hanan looked scary with cuts on her face and her legs and then I saw blood on her pants in between her legs and I got a scary feeling in my belly.

"Are you all right?" I asked her, praying she would say yes and get up, but she cried so hard she couldn't say anything and she didn't move, even when I tried to get her to get up.

The man and woman came from the car that had stopped and were running toward us. "Is anyone hurt?" the man asked as he reached us.

"I think she is," I told him. His wife bent over Hanan, whose face was bright red now. I looked past their car and my heart dropped when I saw my mother running toward us, holding her dress up high enough for her legs to move faster and realized she must have followed us down the road to the street.

"Thank God you are alive!" she gasped. "Hanan! What happened to her?"

"We were going downhill. . . ."

"What were you doing in the street? I told you not to go in the street!" She began yelling about how stupid and foolish and selfish I was for taking someone else into the street, as if it wasn't enough to risk my own life but to take someone else. And more yelling and me just wanting to kick and break my bike and myself for making everything go wrong after it had been so nice.

The couple was from the next village and said that they

would take Hanan to her house; she was still crying as the man carried her off.

I tried to explain what happened to my mother, but she wouldn't listen and I felt so bad at my being so stupid for going in the street and for making Hanan get hurt and for making my mother hate me that I cried. My mother picked up the bike and walked with it in front of me, sometimes turning around to yell how stupid I was or to give me a loud stare. I wished it had been me who had fallen so hard, because for sure Hanan was going to die and it would be my fault for being so stupid to brake when I did.

Hamdi and Fay were very nice to me and told me not to worry about Hanan, that she was fine and that, no, the bike would not be sad. *Sometimes it's best to be wary of people who can see things. . . .*

I didn't see Hanan for a few days. All I could think about was her crying and the blood she had all over the place and how she was probably dead now and that I had killed her. One morning, my mother told me that we were going to Hanan's house to see how she was doing.

"I have to bring her something to apologize with."

My mother stared at me but said nothing.

"I'll take the bike."

"You may not give her your bicycle. That was a present to you from your uncle Hamdi and from Auntie Fay."

"I don't care. She has to have it because it's my fault. I can't ride it anymore. I won't go if I can't take the bicycle."

But my mother surprised me. "We will not go then."

And we didn't. I kept my bicycle and after a few days I couldn't figure out why I had wanted to give it to Hanan in the first place. I still rode it on the little drive by our house and the other kids came over to ride it too. Hanan didn't come to play for a couple of weeks, even though her mother told my mother that she was just fine, just scared by all the bleeding, especially between her legs. My mother explained that there are some places that have lots of blood in them, so they make an injury look worse than it is. "Between your legs is one of those places," she told me. "It's not a good place to have an accident." Hanan didn't have any injuries besides that, only scrapes and scratches.

One funny thing was that her mother saved her bloody underpants and wrapped them in a newspaper from the day we had the accident "so when she gets married, she'll have proof that she's a girl," which I didn't really understand.

"This means Hanan will be married very soon," my mother said, laughing. "Before she knows what she can do with her freedom."

It's funny to think about this memory now. Hanan moved back to the States not long after that. She hasn't gotten married yet, but she is very religious and serious now. Maybe because of what happened, maybe because of her visions, or maybe that's the only way she can keep who she is in big, greedy America. As for Uncle Hamdi, maybe it's just as well he isn't coming. Too bad for Sitti, though. It would have been nice to have her excited by a scrubbed house and a visiting son.

23

....

TRADITIONS

My father is a traditional man, my mother says. That's why he is so strict and why I'm not allowed to talk to boys and why he wants to have more children, even though we are already four—six, if you include Mina and Monia—and my mother can barely manage us as is.

"Like wild dogs," she screams, when we are driving her more crazy than usual. "Like wild dogs with ticks in your asses."

She doesn't say this around my father, though, because he doesn't think women should swear and he'll slap her if she does.

Patsy came for dinner yesterday. Ma cooked *musakhan,* which is my very favorite so I couldn't get mad. She made French fries too, which Patsy couldn't believe.

"You actually *made* these French fries? They're not frozen? You cut them up and everything?"

Ma smiled and nodded, though I didn't think she understood what Patsy said. I started to explain in Arabic, but she interrupted me.

"I understand," she said in English.

Patsy even liked the *musakhan,* though she didn't eat that much, which is probably good because all of the olive oil and onions would give her a stomachache and then she'd hate me.

Then Patsy asked me over for dinner.

"No way," my mother said.

"Why not?"

"I don't know these people, that's why not."

I told Patsy what Ma had said and she suggested that Ma have her whole family over for dinner. Ma liked that idea. "We'll have a barbecue, for the sake of their blue eyes."

Her parents and brother came. Fortunately Auntie Maysoun came too. She speaks English fine and is very good at small talk. Baba was even cheerful.

Finally Ma let me go to Patsy's house for dinner. It was like walking into a TV show.

They have a room where there's a huge television and her father sat in front of it the whole time I was there. He barely said hi or anything, just sat in front of the huge screen and stared.

Her mom came home after we had been there for an hour and she had a huge bucket of fried chicken. I was excited because we never get to eat food from outside.

Patsy has a little brother who is six, like Hamdan. He took one look at his mother and screamed, "Again? We have to eat fried rats again?"

"Shut up, Mickey."

He's named after the singer Mick Jagger.

I told Ma that Patsy had a little brother who was named after a rock musician and she gasped.

"Swear to God," I told her.

"*This* is the problem with America! Instead of naming their children after family or prophets or heroes, they name them after rock stars. Who would believe such a thing?"

I laughed, but she didn't find it funny.

"Do they drink beer in front of you?"

"Who?"

"Batzy's parents."

"No."

My mother was silent. I knew what she was thinking. I knew she was remembering Jennifer, the other American friend I had.

Jennifer lived down the street and went to the same school. Everything in her house was hippie-style, including her tiny bedroom that didn't have a door, just dangling pink beads. She was very nice, but she had an older brother who drank beer at all hours of the day and looked at nasty magazines. The first time I went over there to play, she showed me a stack of them. All of them had naked ladies with huge breasts and I knew that I shouldn't be looking at them.

Jennifer and I played normal games too, but her feet smelled a lot and Ma encouraged us to play outside whenever we were at our house. One day Jennifer wore boots and the stink was so bad that Ma made her leave the shoes outside.

"Deadly. Doesn't she bathe?" Ma said in Arabic while Jennifer was sitting next to me. I pretended not to hear.

When Ma left the room, Jennifer showed me two of her brother's magazines that she had brought over.

I was looking through one of them, and on one page, there were nine small pictures of a blond woman with large lips. In the first picture she wore a white, man's shirt and black pants. In the next picture she wore the same shirt, no pants, and high-heeled black shoes. In the third picture she wore the black pants from the first picture, suspenders, and nothing else. The combination continued until she was naked, except for her high heels and a bow tie, and was resting one foot on a black chair.

For some reason this picture fascinated me, which is why I didn't notice when Ma came in the room. Suddenly she was in front of me.

"What is that?"

Before I could answer, she grabbed it, and after a couple of seconds she screamed curses like I have never heard, and half of which I could not understand.

She looked at Jennifer and screamed in Arabic for her to leave. Jennifer ran out, grabbing her shoes, but not stopping to put them on.

Ma slapped my face, cursed me, cursed America, cursed my father, and cursed God.

She burned the magazines and then dinner, which made Baba angry. But Ma decided not to tell him what I had done. I was not allowed to play with Jennifer after that.

I know this is what Ma was thinking when I told her about Mick and Patsy.

24

....

DRESS UP

*T*o clear my head of Sharif, I decide to visit my mother's uncle, Abu Salwan, and his family in Irbid. My father does not seem surprised, doesn't try to dissuade me, and even offers to drive me there. I prefer to take the bus; it will give me a chance to be alone and think.

Just as I am saying good-bye to my father, Sharif appears. My heart skips a bit as he greets my father.

"I hope I have not, in any way, offended you," he says when my father is out of earshot.

"No, not at all. I just wanted to visit my uncle while I am here." I feel very uncomfortable, as if I'd told a lie and had got caught.

"At least let me drive you," he says, his smooth voice tripping a bit.

I politely refuse his offer and say good-bye, hoping he doesn't notice my clammy hands as we shake.

The bus is not full and I find a seat by the window. My father is out of sight. Sharif is leaning against his car, watching. I cannot see straight and my face feels hot.

The driver announces our departure. I wave at Sharif, who nods. Even as we drive, my thoughts are filled with Sharif and his punching bag and his strong arms, and his poems. Is this what it is like to leave a lover? Ridiculous thoughts. And then, as though I am watching an Indian movie, Sharif's black Fiat appears next to the bus. He looks out of the window and up at me.

Following, following, no smiles. And then, finally, he pulls to the side of the road, gets out and watches the bus go. I turn my head at an impossible angle and watch until he is out of sight.

When I get off the Hijazi bus at the central bus terminal in Irbid, Abu Salwan is waiting for me. We drive the short distance to their house just outside one of the refugee camps.

Abu Salwan and his wife had one son and one daughter. The son is married and lives in the Gulf. The daughter married, had a daughter, and then died in childbirth with a second child, who also died. Her husband also worked in the Gulf and his parents were very old, so Abu Salwan and his wife raised Fawziyya, who is a few years older than I am.

Upstairs to the sitting room, then *mensef* to feast on, then the photo albums come out. The afternoon passes with vague memories embracing me. I see pictures of my mother I have never seen before. She looks young and happy and so very healthy. And pictures of the last time I was with this family, when they picked me up and took me to Petra, even though it was the middle of the tourist season.

My mother never visited Petra. She said that one time when she was in the States, she and Hamdi had gone to his professor's house for dinner. He was German and very well traveled. When he learned they were Palestinian, he talked of his visits to Jordan, mostly about Petra. "You must climb the stairs to the top," he told them. "You must go *up to the top where the rocks meet the sky*. The Nabateans have a place of sacrifice there. It is so incredible."

My mother had always hoped to go, but for some reason never did.

Imagine that people built this city in the rocks and actually lived here!

"Abu Salwan, can we climb to the top?" I ask.

He turns to his granddaughter. "Fawziyya, take your cousin Hala up those stairs. Let's see how far you can go."

And so we climb, though it is not proper for two girls to be racing up steps with foreigners. Abu Salwan turns his lips inside his mouth to keep his words from coming out; he is a good host first, an uncle second.

We climb, my Bedouin cousin and I. Not too long after we start, we both stop to rest. I am already so tired I consider turning around, but if I don't go now, I probably never will, so Fawziyya—obliging me because I am her guest and her responsibility—and I continue up the mountain with twists and turns and big steps, more than a thousand of them, and my feet touch each one.

All the people coming down are foreign and they all smile and say hello in English, and I answer each one because I have been around Americans so much. I think Fawziyya sees me as too western, but she goes along with everything and even says hi to the few women who pass us. I have never sweated more or felt air hotter. I worry about Fawziyya, but she giggles at the freedom.

Finally, we reach the top. Fawziyya and I stop and stare. We are young, fit, totally out of breath and drenched in sweat, and in front of us there is a hundred-year-old hunched-over lady who has chairs and tables set up and is selling sodas from under an umbrella.

"She must have a secret way up," Fawziyya says as soon as she can catch her breath.

We drink warm Pepsis and stand before the actual Place of Sacrifice: a circle of mud raised among stones and covered with markers.

I look beyond it and see the rocks still go up higher. "Maybe there is something more," I say, and Fawziyya follows me up, up, but it's not steep like the steps; this time it is just a smooth slant of gray-black-purple rocks that look like nothing I have seen before. We are higher than anything else. We are looking down on the tops of the other mountains. My cousin suddenly holds me close to her hot body, perhaps thinking I am going to fall off the edge. We are in the sky so high that we are on the same level as the blue, and when we sit down, we see a lizard, as big as my arm and clear blue, the color of the sky.

"He wants to fit in," Fawziyya says. We stare at it awhile, willing it to come closer, but it gets tired of us and goes between the rocks.

My shirt is drenched and sticky and it makes me feel sick and clammy. I look around and can see no one—so far that it seems we are the only living creatures, except for the lizard and for God. It is completely quiet, so we will hear if someone comes. I take off my shirt and bra and then my pants as well. Fawziyya just stares at me.

"What are you doing?" she practically shouts. "What if someone sees you?"

"Who is going to see me? Besides, it's so quiet that we'll hear if anyone comes this way."

I don't say anything else, but as I lay my clothes out flat on the rocks to dry, my cousin strips down to her underpants, bra, and undershirt, and lies back slowly on a rock, letting her skin get used to its heat. We let the sun tickle us for what seems like hours, but is probably five or ten minutes—long enough that our clothes dry. When we come back down again, my legs feet like rubber bands. We find Abu Salwan sitting in the shade with two Bedouin men.

"Thank God you are back safely. How was it?" Abu Salwan asks.

"I have never seen anything more beautiful," I say. "And we saw the most incredible lizard!"

Abu Salwan and the two men nod, perhaps so used to foreigners that they can approve of our exploration even though it isn't proper, and I feel ashamed. This is not my father. I don't want him to be offended. Perhaps I have stretched the limits of his hospitality. (If only he knew what we did at the top of the mountain!) The entire drive home and into the night, we talk of the blue lizard, the old woman, and the sky we stood in.

It is the next evening, and like every night I spend with them, Abu Salwan tells a story. This one, however, is about my mother, "when she was about the same age that you are now.

"Even though it was many years ago, rarely a day passes that I don't think of your mother," he says. "It is because of her that I gave my son the biggest beating of his life." He is silent for a moment and I hear the hum of too many families on top of one another.

It was so many years ago and your father had just dropped your mother to spend the weekend with us. My daughter, may God have mercy on her, was still alive. It was afternoon, blue sky like that lizard on the rocks in Petra, hot like wanting to be inside a watermelon, and Friday like peaceful after prayers, after eating, everybody wanting to rest.

Everybody except Salwan, Huda, and Saara, my daughter.

Salwan is twelve and Saara is fourteen. Huda is nineteen.

I had visitors that day. "Out of the sitting room, out of the hallway, cover your hair, girl," I shout. Even Salwan shouldn't come in.

The children saw them coming down the road toward our house and somehow knew they were coming to see me, so they ran inside to tell me.

"Yaba," they shouted in my ears, though they are old enough to know better. "Yaba, two men with knives and guns are here."

The four of us got to the window just in time to see the two men reaching the gate to our house. I looked across the alley to the apartment building and I saw some of our neighbors envying our important visitors, especially that old Indian lady who is Christian and thinks she is better than us even though she lives in the same stinky alley as we do.

"Yaba, why are they dressed like that?" All in black, so serious with their weapons, just like the pictures we have in the sitting room from when I was young, *when men were noble*.

"My dear," I tell Saara, putting my hand on her head to stop her thoughts from running out her mouth like a snake, "these men are guards, Bedouin guards from Petra."

As they make their way up the stairs, I send the kids to the back of the house, away from the formal sitting room, away from the regular sitting room. The girls help my wife as she makes tea and puts cakes on a tray and Salwan lingers out on the balcony to see if any of his friends are outside. The afternoon is filled with talk and shouts and calls for more tea and more food and Um Salwan putting everything outside the door, then knocking and going back to the kitchen before the door opens, before any eyes can see her.

And then quiet, not even street noises sneaking in. Um

Salwan is sound asleep in the bedroom and Salwan and Saara and Huda are awake as can be.

"Let's see if they are sleeping," Salwan says.

"But what if they aren't?" says Huda.

"I'll go first," he volunteers.

They sneak down the hall, Salwan in front, their feet bare on the cool tile floor. Sneak, sneak, Salwan pushes open the door slowly slowly and then looks in before turning back to Saara and Huda, and soon three faces are peering at me as I sit in the corner reading the Quran. My guests are asleep: on either side of the room is a figure, each man covered from head to toe in his black robe.

"Do you think they are dead?" Saara asks, and I wave her away so as not to wake anyone up.

What followed, I learned later.

"Do you want to go outside and play?" Saara says to Huda and Salwan, and their feet take them back down the cool hallway.

The three are bored as they go through the formal sitting room on their way to the large patio to play underneath the grape vines. Salwan stops as his eyes catch hold of something on the small mother-of-pearl table: two leather belts with holsters, each one with a gun and a knife.

"Don't touch them," Huda says.

"But those men are asleep."

"They might wake up, and besides, you are too young to be touching guns."

"They won't wake up for a while, and besides, I know how to use a gun," argues Salwan and carefully picks up one of the heavy belts and wraps it around his waist. He is so thin that it goes around twice. Saara looks scared, but she puts on the other belt. My two children go back to the hallway and stand in front of the large mirror, admiring themselves.

Huda—who is so much older than they are, in years and also because she has lived abroad and is a married woman—ignores them at first, but when they go out to the patio, she follows. Suddenly Salwan and Saara are Bedouin of the same tribe, ready to fight the enemy, deaf to Huda's protests. They take their knives out of their sheaths and stab imaginary attackers. They dance like this, slaying countless invisible enemies until Salwan stops and pulls out his gun. Saara does the same.

The gun is heavy and cold in Salwan's hands and feels nice, important. He looks up and points his gun at Saara, his finger on the trigger, though she is not the enemy, even in their game. All of a sudden, Huda realizes that this gun is probably loaded, and she shouts at Salwan to put it down, which startles him. There is a huge crack and Saara falls, more from the noise and fear than from the pain in her shoulder.

The world wakes up and time moves in fast and slow motion at the same time. Salwan is frozen, looking first at the large hole that has exploded in the wall around the patio behind Saara and then at Huda, who is bent over Saara and screaming at Salwan to get help. Blood is spilling on the patio floor.

I ran out when I heard the shot, and my mouth cannot stop the cursing at my foolish son who is still holding the gun. My friends, awakened by the noise, run out to see what is happening.

I bend over Saara, still cursing, but then saying nice things so she won't be scared. I take off my *kaffiyah* and push it against her shoulder which makes her scream. Then Um Salwan comes out screaming and wailing. I tell her to stop, that the bullet only grazed her shoulder: *See, there it is in the wall over there.*

Then I remember the gun and go to Salwan, my words soft

at first, asking him for the gun, which he hands over without a word. The gun was like his shield and the minute it is out of his hands, my curses and fists are covering his body and Salwan doesn't move, just drops limp like a bag of rice that's pouring itself out, and soon I stop hitting him and push him toward the house.

My wife and Huda are still crumpled over Saara. My wife is taking off the belt with rough hands and whispering nice things and begging God to let her live.

"We've got to take her to the hospital," Huda keeps saying.

So many words fill the loud air as I carry Saara downstairs to my truck with Um Salwan and the two Bedouin men following behind us, she whispering prayers over and over and the Bedouin men shouting and whispering and me answering.

God forgive me for having been so careless with such a dangerous weapon.

God forgive their stupidity. They are foolish children. Nothing happened, thank God and thank you for your concern.

Please forgive my carelessness.

I can feel the neighbors' eyes and words following us. *What are you looking at, you foolish weasel?* I ask my friends to please stay and watch Salwan and then we drive to the gray-yellow hospital on Sharia Filisteen.

Salwan told me later they played cards with him and told him stories, which would have made me furious had I not already reached my limits of rage and given him the beating of his life, so bad that he almost had to go to the hospital on Sharia Filisteen too.

What made me remember this story today is the oddest thing of all. Your mother came back for a visit a few months later.

Saara was showing her the scar on her shoulder. Huda was turning her head this way, and then that way, for a couple of minutes, and then she laughed.

"Why are you laughing?" we all asked her.

"Abu Salwan, this scar is in the shape of a lizard. It is nothing if it is not a lizard."

So you see, Hala and Fawziyya, that lizard you saw in Petra was a reminder that your mothers are always with you.

25

....

BACKGAMMON

*T*his is my last night. A week and a half has passed in the blink of an eye.

The sun has been gone awhile and the night's cool winds cover us as we sit beneath the grapevines on the balcony. Remnants of the day's laundry dangle amid a circle of cans filled with flowers of exotic smells in an alley that usually reeks of sewage.

A wrinkled hand pushes a black chip across the felt.

The crickets are in symphony.

Um Salwan comes and sits next to me, a hand on each knee and a smile for her husband.

"Come on," I say. "Let's walk."

"Tomorrow, girl. Tomorrow we will walk to the university and back."

This has become our joke: I wanted to walk to the university that is more than a mile away and Um Salwan coughs after two alleys, but she swears she will walk with me tomorrow, God willing.

Crack, crack, crack, say pumpkin seeds between teeth as

cracked as the shells they are biting and nowhere near as white. *Ping,* onto the dish that piles itself higher and higher.

"I will go to sleep now," I say.

Concentration is broken momentarily as protests heavier than the chips on felt are piled on my head.

"It is too early," Fawziyya shouts next to me and clutches my shoulder.

I am convinced and silence returns with occasional pings and cracks and growls of passing cars. Sleep can wait, though Abu Salwan will let me go if I insist more than twice.

"Abu Salwan, tell me about the gold. . . ."

Eyes flash and a smile unfolds.

"I have told the story."

Click, of chips hitting against one another; victory is once again in the court of age and wisdom.

"I know, Abu Salwan, but tell me again. Please."

He laughs. "Oh, Miss Professor, you always want stories."

I nod. They call me Miss Professor now because I will be starting university soon and because I ask too many questions. Um Salwan and Fawziyya laugh, knowing that Abu Salwan will indulge me. He is, after all, Abu Qisas, Father of Stories.

Leaning back in his chair, he begins:

"As you know, my child, my tribe is from the Galilee area. Some people from our tribe led a settled life, but some of us still traveled—in our case it was between the Galilee and Irbid. We did this until 1948, when the war broke out and bad luck had us on the eastern side of the river, forbidden by the new Israeli government to return more than once a year."

Fawziyya gets up.

"Where are you escaping to?"

"Grandfather, I know this story and it needs tea to accompany it." She picks two mint leaves from a paint can filled with the herb and goes inside.

Abu Salwan continues:

"As you also know, I often worked as a driver for the Baraka Company, transporting various merchandise to and from Iraq. There were two routes: via the heavily traveled paved road, or following the paved road for a bit, then cutting through the desert. Most men stayed on the paved road for its reliability and population, but if you were in a hurry, going through the desert was the best way: slow driving, but a much shorter distance, which is why the Baraka Company liked to hire Bedouin drivers. We are loyal and we know the desert.

"They'd say that inexperienced drivers—those men from the villages who wanted to make more money or were in a hurry to return—sometimes took the desert shortcuts. There are many stories of mysterious disappearances, though I think most were robberies."

Fawziyya appears with a tray and small glasses of sugared tea—I can see the line of white at the bottom—and places a glass in front of each of us.

"Since I knew the desert region well, I usually chose it if I had a good truck because it was much quicker. This one time, however, I had a truck that I did not trust at all. If you broke down on the road, there would always be someone to help you, but if you broke down in the desert, you were left to your own devices. There was no hurry for this shipment, so I took the paved road. Don't think 'paved' meant what it does today, either. The road was bumpy and dusty and crowded and was always a challenge to your truck and your patience, especially in the summer months when the sun set your skin on fire.

"I reached Iraq without incident, and was getting in my truck to go to sleep for the night when I heard a voice calling me. I leaned out of the truck to find the dispatcher for the Baraka Company running toward me.

"'Please,' he told me. 'I have a shipment that must get back as soon as possible. The only way it will get there on time is by leaving now, and you are the only Bedouin driver here.'

"I have never shunned a job so I agreed that I would make a pot of strong coffee and would be on my way, in spite of my rickety truck.

"It was springtime and the stars filled the black sky. There is nothing like the vastness of the desert to make a man's mind wander and perhaps steer him away from his intended direction. One should not underestimate man's need for sleep, either.

"Despite the coffee and the clear sky, not long after I pulled off the highway to take the desert route, I found myself facing an unfamiliar direction on an unfamiliar stretch of desert with cracked ground, sparse bushes, and an occasional tree. I stopped the truck and got out because I can always reorient myself if I am standing on the ground. I looked at the sky. How could I be facing south when I should be driving west? I got back in the truck and veered so that I was driving northwest. The more I drove the more worried I became. I had never seen this territory before, and while I would probably find my way out if I were to continue, I might run into a Bedouin encampment that I did not know. Who knows? With the night and the headlights, they might not be welcoming. I wrestled with this for some time—I had a very good reputation as a driver and I did not want to risk that, but at the same time, I am not easily disoriented and yet here I was lost in the middle of a strange desert. No, I decided, better to wait until daylight, which was only a few hours away, even if it meant the shipment would be late. Certainly it would be better to have it late than not to get it there at all.

"I looked ahead and saw a small range of hills and a couple of trees. I will settle there for the night and continue at the break of dawn, I decided. I pulled my truck over and parked the passenger side flush with the base of a tree so that no one could sneak up on me from the other door. I got a flashlight and left the truck to relieve myself. I passed the light over the base of the hills and was startled to see a piece of wood the size of a large window.

"How odd, I thought, that such a piece of wood could make its way into this part of the desert. I leaned over to lift it, and what a surprise I had to see a ladder leading down. As I leaned in and waved my flashlight around, all I could see was the floor immediately below the ladder, maybe five feet down. And then I had another surprise: a bright red Bedouin-style carpet lay on the floor. I realized that this must be someone's house and that I was intruding. '*As-salaamu alaykum!*' I shouted into the cave. No answer came, but I was not convinced, so I repeated my greeting and was answered by a faint echo. I felt a chill about me.

"I climbed down the small ladder and into the cave. My flashlight danced off the mud walls. There were several brass coffeepots and rugs piled in a corner. I went to unroll one of the rugs, just to look at it, and I felt that it was covering something. I lifted up carpet after carpet and found underneath a wooden crate. There was no lock on it and the lid lifted up easily. I will never forget the shock I felt as I shined my light on its contents: gold gold gold. This crate, large enough to hold a baby, was filled to the top with bracelets, necklaces, rings, and coins of gold, all twenty-two or twenty-four carat. I have never seen anything like it and I thought I must be dreaming, that I had taken leave of my senses and I was now hallucinating. But it was true. I put my hand in and the further I burrowed, the more spectacular the gold pieces became, covered with ornate carvings and twists and etchings.

"This was booty from the time of the Prophet himself, God bless him and grant him salvation. There is no such thing today. I began to think of all the things I could do with this gold.

"I decided to go back to my truck. God forbid someone should come along and steal it and leave me stranded. I took a large ring with me. It was large for my forefinger and I turned it round and round as if it were *masbaha*.

"As I sat in the cab of my truck, under a blanket that barely kept the cold out, I thought of the gold. To this day I cannot tell you whether what followed was a dream or reality. I was again kneeling in front of the crate of gold, trying to put some of it in bags, when a jumpy little monkeylike creature with long pointy ears appeared. The *ifreet*, moving in a cloud of dust, bounced on the crate and said, 'It is not yet time for you to take this gold. There are Bedouin on this land who know nothing of the gold, but if you take it, they will see you and they will find the gold on you, steal it, and kill you for it. You must wait.'

"I shuddered, perhaps from sleep. I still had the ring on my finger and the sun was just getting ready to come up over the horizon. I got out of my truck, washed my hands and feet in the sand, faced southeast, and prayed. When I was through, my mind was clear and I remembered the night before. I knew that I could not take the gold and come out alive, so I decided to leave it in God's hands and come back again.

"I drove and before long I saw the black tents of the Bedouin from a distance, but no one approached me. I found my way back to the paved highway and raced along with my shipment. Fortunately for me, no one was awake enough to get angry that the shipment was a couple of hours late.

"When I returned home, I told no one of the Bedouin, of

the gold, or of the dream. I decided that if the *ifreet* ever returned, I would call upon my two most trusted friends and
we would go together to get the gold, which we would split
evenly. This happened many years ago. Three months ago the
ifreet came to me in a dream and told me that he was no
longer guarding it, that it was rightly mine. . . ."

"Abu Salwan, why don't you get the gold?"

"My dear, there is some sort of military exercise in the
area where the cave is. They will be there for a while, though
I don't believe forever. We must wait until they are done and
gone or they will not allow us to leave without taking the
booty and claiming it is government property."

What comes next is my favorite part of the story.

Abu Salwan has a thin leather cord around his neck that
disappears beneath his gelabiyya. He pulls at it and at the end
is a large, gold ring. He fingers it absently.

I want the story to continue.

"Abu Salwan!"

"What's wrong?"

"You didn't tell us enough about the *ifreet*."

"I did. I told you the *ifreet* came to me and told me I could
not take the gold and—"

"Describe him, please!"

"Oh, I see, my child." Abu Salwan leans forward and
looks in my eyes. "This *ifreet* was disguised," he says in a
quiet voice. The alley is quiet now too. "It was long, longer
than a man's foot. It was thin as a child's wrist, black as
the night . . . and with as many legs as all of the villagers
together."

Fawziyya and I look at each other and then at Abu
Salwan, who wears a sneaky smile. "This is not the *ifreet* we
know, Abu Salwan."

"I told you, my girls, this *ifreet* was disguised to look like some sort of creature." His voice is a whisper now. "And it seems that the *ifreet* has come to visit us."

He points to a spot not three feet from where we are sitting, where a giant millipede wanders across the floor.

Screams break the silence of the night, followed by the deep laugh of a man who knows stories as well as he knows the desert and its creatures.

PART THREE

26

....

SLEEPING OVER

*P*atsy asked me to a slumber party, and when I asked Ma she refused.

"You are not going to sleep anywhere outside this family until the day you are married."

I didn't argue. I knew that was what she was going to say. And even if she had said yes, Baba would probably have hit me just for asking.

When I told Patsy, she laughed. "How are you ever going to have sex with a boy if you always have to sleep at home?"

I felt funny, like she was laughing at me. I had never thought about sex with a boy before I got married. I know that American girls do that, and probably even my cousin Soraya, but that's different.

Baba yells so much, mostly at the boys. He only gets mad at me if he's been drinking or when I do something really bad—like the time he caught me with my brother and my cousin Tariq in the closet lighting matches. It wasn't even one of those big closets, but I guess we were so small we all fit nice and cozy. We were pretending that we were in the woods having a campfire.

When Baba found us, he yelled, "You are the shame of this family, trying to burn the house around you. Your mothers would have been better off if they had goats instead of you children!"

He got Muhammad first and hit him all over with his belt, and then Tariq. Both of them were screaming. Then he hit me with the belt and I screamed and cried for hours.

He yells at Ma a lot too. Ma just stands there and mutters words I don't understand. I feel sorry for her.

Scary is the rumor started by my brother, Muhammad, whose two dollars I took to buy a barrette, that he saw me at school kissing Michael behind the gym at lunch and having Baba not believe me because he doesn't have any reason to.

Scary is when the yelling doesn't stop and when everyone has bruises "from the Devil," as my mother says. I know better. I know they come because the sand sends him inside that small bottle of liquor he keeps locked in his toolbox and turns his insides into fire.

SORAYA

27

....

LOVE STORY/REMEMBERING STORY

Like I said, I can make any man talk. That includes my crazy uncle Haydar. I know his truth. He fed it to me once. So long ago and it is still my secret.

Once upon a time, a sad young man ran across the sea, away from talks that drowned him drunk, like a dead bird in a shit-filled fountain.

"Questions need not be asked in my arms. Eyes and feet are all that change the world, besides the obvious," he'd tell his girlfriends, whose laughter painted him clever as well as slick, shiny-shoed, and charming: quite exotic by their standards, even as he aged and aged and filled his shoes with lifts and insoles.

In Arizona his sad eyes swallowed clouds and shut, so he could keep them always there. Memories floated fat and still above his head, no matter how fast he ran or how full his arms were with sweet delight and youth.

"Running can't go on forever," he read in a fortune cookie to the same little girl who asked him why he was so alone and had no one in his life, and why he hardly ever visited; and wherever did he get those heavy eyes and flying feet?

Walking home, he kicked stones under a southwest sky, brighter than skies he remembers.

"But you are my uncle and I don't even know you well," the girl replied after he asked her to come to him. "Except that you always ask me how I am, like you want to know the answer, but I can't break a rule like that, not tonight at least."

Some days, weeks, months later during another visit, she risked it all and went to the running man. "In your arms I am beautiful and I can fly," she whispered on his sweaty neck, her words sliding down his chest.

A lifetime later, lying in bed, his eyes facing the moon, he felt fear come visit.

"Why are you scared? Did you hear a noise?" she had asked, but his eyes were silent. He held her so tight in his arms her breath was hard to find.

He hated the noises that brought memories in the blackness of night, when he longed to be strong as he had been, stronger than the night that covered him in its heavy blanket of still pictures.

Rain, then silence in a boy's ears, and suddenly all is lost before it begins. On that night, long after it began between the too young girl and the running man, he told her his story, which was also her story:

One clear, black, after-the-rain night when he was a boy in that big house in that little village, some men came and took his father—her grandfather—away and killed him in the valley, "practically beneath my mother's window." He saw their faces, for they were faces he saw every day, but he was so young, he could not cover his tongue with their names.

It ate and ate his soul away. For a time, he stopped seeing.

And then he taught himself to run and run and almost fly. He ran and ran, forever and faster than anyone and then he ran across the ocean, but not before he painted the sky with the blood of those men who took everything away.

Rain, then silence pounding on the rooftops over his sister's broken face that stared out into the valley. Huda, why have you opened the window? Yama, what has happened?

"But who were they? Why did they do that?"

He held her tighter, trying to be a blanket for her with his running body, now so very, very still.

"I'm sure your mother, my sister, with her golden tongue, has told you stories of our father. He had land and ideas. He brought so much into the village from outside and there were those who did not want that. I have done an awful thing. So long ago, and still it seems like yesterday."

"I can glue sins and secrets under my tongue," she said.

"I have told this to no one else, and you are so young to bear this burden."

Her tiny body holds him close, her tears like holy water spilling. "I will love you always," she whispers and he feels the years of running whispers and the relief of a burden going away.

Very clear, the shapes in the bedroom, and the fear blanket is pushed slowly, slowly to the end of the bed, at least for now.

28

....

MOTHERS

*E*ven though it's summer, it's raining so hard that it sounds like big men running back and forth on our roof. I hate the rain.

Baba's mother died twenty years ago today.

"Maybe that's why it's raining so hard," I said.

"Maybe." He seems sad today, quiet and gloomy.

Ma feels bad too. I know that she's thinking about her own mother.

I have never met either of my grandmothers.

I finally have a secret, but it's an ugly secret and I'm not sure what to do with it.

Ma always used to tell my two half sisters about boys, especially American boys, and how they will take that secret thing between your legs for nothing. "No committer." That's why Mina and Monia were married so young. I think it's also because their father, my mother's first husband, was dead, and Baba wanted to get rid of the problem of unmarried girls in his house.

"Your husband has to be the one to take it from you," Ma told me once. "Otherwise you are a disgrace to us and we are stuck with you forever." Then she said, in English, "You shameful."

One day I went over to Patsy's house after school. Her parents weren't there and the house felt quiet with no television on. I was surprised when the doorbell rang and Michael was there. At first I was happy to see him, but then I got a funny feeling and went back to the dining-room table to work on my homework. He was looking at Patsy funny and it seemed like he was someone else.

"We're going to go study in the back, okay, Kadeeja?" Patsy said, without even looking at me.

My ugly-sounding name sounded uglier than usual, and it seemed strange to me that she had me over but then was going to study in another room, but I said okay. I don't know how much time passed, but I started to feel panicky when I didn't hear any noise. I went toward her parents' bedroom, which is all pink and purple. I was in there a couple of times before when we jumped up and down on the waterbed. The door was closed so I knocked on it. At first there was no answer, but then I knocked again, and Michael said, "Come in, Khadija." (One of the reasons I like him is because he says my name how it's supposed to be said.)

I don't know what I was expecting to see, but it wasn't Michael and Patsy under the covers in the waterbed.

"Is everything okay?"

"Yeah, Kadeeja," Patsy said. "Just leave us alone, okay?"

I turned away and shut the door behind me. I felt horrible, like can't-see and can't-think kind of horrible. My books were all over the place and I couldn't stuff them in my bag fast enough. I ran from her front door to our house. Thinking about what I saw made me feel dirty, like when you go by a car crash and look by accident and on purpose at the same time, but then you feel sick because of what you saw.

When I got home, my mother was playing with little Hamouda, who is two and a half years old. When I saw them I started to cry.

"What's wrong, little cucumber? Are you sick?"

"Sick, sick," said Hamouda.

My mother hugged me and felt my forehead.

"I think I'm getting sick," I told her. "Lots of the kids at school are sick," I lied.

"You stay home with us and we'll make you better, won't we, Hamouda."

Hamouda looked at me and shouted, "Yes!"

Two days later, my safe mother flew a million miles away to see her dying mother. My uncle Hamdi paid for her ticket.

"I promise you, *habibti*, only for one week." But I knew she was lying because I heard Baba say two weeks and no more.

"Let me come, Ma, please," I begged.

"No, *habibti*. You have to stay to keep an eye on the boys. Go to Maysoun if it gets bad." But I knew Baba wouldn't let me. He would expect me to take care of everything.

I cried and cried, because without her our house is empty. Even Baba feels it.

29

....

MAZIUNA

Months have passed in a blink. Days take forever. My world has flipped upside down. My father is dead and my grandmother, with whom we now live, has gotten old so quickly. Something in her has walked away, and now my auntie Shahira is visiting, to help my mother and also to help with my grandmother. And I am still watching, like my mother taught me to do.

The seventy-four-year-old woman named Maziuna sits at the edge of her bed, her face decorated with angry wrinkles and spots like bruises. She wears a scarf that's red and streaked with gold and she does not recognize her daughter, who has come to visit after so many years away, only the second time since she remarried and she and her two daughters, Mina and Monia, left for America.

There are many heavy women who punctuate the room. They are all somehow related. The daughter who is visiting vies hardest for her mother's attention, whispering, singing, and talking to her, and when she gets no response, shouting.

Still, Maziuna is oblivious as Omar Diyab serenades them from a boombox.

The visiting daughter, Shahira, does not give up. She props her mother's face between her palms and shouts, "Where is that mule Shahira? Have you seen her?" Her mother looks just over her daughter's left shoulder and stares at nothing, or maybe at a memory she just peeled off the windowsill and let drop and break.

"Ma, Ma, where is that mule Shahira?" She forces her mother's face toward her own, but the eyes are still looking over there, under the window, at the floor.

Sahar, hiding her own grief today, comes and rests her body on the other side of their mother. They let her be for a while, but when a lively song begins to play, they shake her to the beat of the music. Hennaed orange hair sneaks from beneath the gypsy scarf. "Come on, dance," they say, and push and turn her, but the eyes are still stuck on the floor, and then the window, and maybe far beyond.

Later in the day, more visitors and children drift in and out. Omar Diyab is still singing and the television is also on. A neighbor has a video camera so that the visiting sister will have something to take back besides memories.

"Look, Amti, look at the camera," he says, and a boy in an orange shirt stands behind Maziuna and twists her gypsied head toward the camera. Her eyes don't meet the lens, but the man behind the camera is satisfied and turns to focus on the children in front of the television. Shahira serves too sweet tea, though she is the visitor, and then goes to sit on the bed next to her mother. This time she does not say anything to her and does nothing to get her attention.

The walls of this house are as thick as a married woman's waist and in the summer, when people come to visit, it is cool inside, floating memories of a livelier time.

Sahar, a cheerful woman in spite of her hardships, flops on the bed on the other side of Maziuna. "How are you, Ma?"

Maziuna turns to her and splits her lips apart to smile, showing her teeth, some gold, some missing. "Hello, chickie!" she shouts with sharpness that makes the two boys in front of the television turn around.

"Did you hear that?" shouts Sahar across their mother to Shahira.

Sahar, the eldest living daughter, is now a widow. She is living once again in her mother's house because her late husband's brothers kicked her out of the house she shared with her husband, the house in which she had lived for all of her adult life. They told her that she and her only daughter had no right to it.

"Did you hear that, sister Shahira? My mother is still calling me 'chickie'!" Laughter clatters around the room, but Shahira's eyes do not dance like her sister's eyes. "Chickie" was once reserved for her.

Maziuna is silent again and stares at the television with the same stare as the two little boys. Conversation comes in shouts over the electronics that dot the room until the nephew turns off the tape player.

"How do you find America?" Um Radwan asks Shahira, whose hand rests on her mother's knee.

"It's very scary sometimes, Um Radwan, though thank God we are doing all right. It's very easy to miss your family there—no one is friendly and the cities can be very dangerous. Things could be worse though. Life is made of good and bad."

"There are some who would say it is entirely bad," says Um Radwan. The children are chased out of the room by the women's disappointments and by the loud neighbor who has no soft words for anyone.

"What is this burden that God has given us to bear?" says Um Radwan.

"It's the will of God and we must endure," says Sahar.

"The worst part of it is that my children talk like Americans," Shahira says, opening up the stories the other women have been waiting for. "Even the two older girls, the ones born here, they live like Americans, always busy and no time ever, and there is nothing I can do to change that."

"What a shame."

She waits to continue.

"My husband is very difficult at times and does not respect people, not even his own father. Oof, you should hear the way he talks to him, just like an American. I mean no respect at all," Shahira says, glancing at her sister, who is listening quietly. "What a shame," she says.

"When I went to America with my two little daughters, I was not foolish enough to believe that everything would be like a fairy tale, but I did think I would find some comfort in life." Shahira pauses for a moment, turning to her mother, but her mother's eyes are nowhere near looking into hers, and are well beyond worrying about the sadness stitched into her daughter's face.

"It is very difficult to live among strangers and more difficult when those strangers are your own children." She stares at the television and her sister nods in sympathy.

The visit only lasts two weeks—"How can I stay longer when I have four children to take care of?"—despite the protests of her sister, who begs her to stay another month. Before Shahira leaves, she and her sister go to Jerusalem with a video camera so she can take her country home, give it to her children in a way they will take it.

"Next time, God willing, you will stay for much longer

and you will bring all your children with you," says Sahar as Shahira is saying good-bye to everyone.

Bajis and his van are waiting and Shahira goes to sit with her mother one more time before she leaves. No one else is in the room and Shahira is quiet as she looks at the gypsy scarf that ties up the remains of her mother's hair.

"Ma, I'm going now."

Maziuna turns to look at her, but then looks away as though not recognizing her grown-up daughter.

"Ma, please take care of yourself."

Maziuna is staring out the window again.

Shahira grasps her mother's frail body in an awkward sideways hug. "If only you could see my life now. You would never believe it. I live in such a different world now. I think it would have been better if Monia and Mina and I stayed here, stayed with you like I wanted to. If only you hadn't thought that marriage was the only answer." Shahira looks at the window that has her mother's attention. "Of course, that would mean no tribe of little boys and no Khadija. If only you could see her. She is like a little boy with all her energy and stubbornness." Again, Shahira stares at the window that looks out over the valley.

"Khadija played in corn," Maziuna says in a squeaky voice and Shahira stares at her mother as if this is the first time she sees her.

"What?"

"Chickie!" she shouts, and just as she says this Sahar comes in the room.

"I'm right here, Ma," she says.

Shahira folds herself up and kisses her mother's forehead before she leaves the room for good. Time to go, she says to herself. Time to go.

One end-of-the-summer day, not long after the old woman's faraway daughter came to see her, the sky is glorious blue.

Not long after the minaret has called Nawara to pray for the first of five times, the old woman wakes up and waits for her daughter to wash her, to dress her in the soft white gown with the flowers embroidered around the neck, and to wrap a scarf around her head. During all these proceedings, the old woman will hold on to her daughter's shoulders or arms, eyes wandering off.

The chores are done and the daughter brings her mother bread and yogurt and urges her to eat, and for a change the old woman obliges her, maybe hoping for some peace. After breakfast, she gets up on her own and goes to the window, where she rests her elbows, her body relaxing as the warm air pours in. Eyes start with the orange trees, whose perfume still finds its way to her window, and then move to the shepherd who is on time as he leads his goats onto the far corner of her land. She closes her eyes to make the pictures stay and then opens them again to get more.

The old woman with her head tied up in a gypsy scarf is tired today, tired like wanting to be water and stretch out in the sun. Her thoughts are interrupted by Mawal, her gentle granddaughter, who comes into the room and greets her, just as she does most mornings.

"*As-salaamu alaykum*, Sitti," she says and comes over to kiss her grandmother on the hand.

The old woman stares. She likes this girl, this young lady with good manners who always smells of soap.

The girl stands with her at the window. After a few quiet moments, she turns and says in a voice that will not interrupt the morning, "I want to tell you a story, Sitti."

They walk to the bed and the old woman lies down, something she does not often do so early in the day. The girl settles her oversized body beside her, leaning back against the pillows and taking her grandmother's hand in hers and rubbing it.

"They say—it may be true, it may not be—that there was a young boy named Jamal who lived in Jerusalem and threw stones at the soldiers one day. The soldiers saw him do this and began chasing him, but he was young and fast so he eluded them as he raced through the Old City, dodging tourists and women with their groceries and all the merchants who stood around trying to sell their wares."

The old woman turns her head so she is facing the window as her granddaughter's words pour gently into her ear.

"He was running everywhere, down this alley and then down that alley. His cheeks were getting hotter and one of his legs was starting to ache, but he kept running anyway. Then he turned down an alley and stopped at the end because it was a courtyard and there was no exit. He panicked because he could hear the shouts of the soldiers not far behind him, but he was not alone in this courtyard, which was actually the back of someone's house. There was also a woman around the age of his mother, wearing an old *roza* that was pulled up, showing her loose *shalwar* pants. She was bent over a vat filled with suds and next to her sat a fat basket of clothes."

The old woman turns and watches her granddaughter as she speaks, wondering at her clear eyes that dance as they tell this story.

"Fear ate the little boy's breath as he stood before her and whispered, 'Hide me.' The woman's eyes were thick with kohl and the sound of boots made her frown. Before an eye could blink, she stripped Jamal naked and pushed him into the soapy water, shoving his telltale red shirt beneath him, hidden from view. She began singing as she washed him, forcing her voice to be ironed smooth, which was how the soldiers found her a moment later when they clamored into the courtyard and shouted at her, 'Where is the kid who ran through here?' They asked her again and again, but she forced her face to look irritated and nothing more than that. They searched around her house as she poured love songs in whispers on Jamal, who quivered with fear while her hands prodded him harshly as his own mother's would. The men in green stomped around, their hands moist on their guns. 'You are sure you didn't see anyone trying to flee?' they asked her again, but her silence chased them off.

"When he was sure the soldiers were gone, Jamal got out of the vat and dried himself, embarrassed to be naked in front of this woman who then gave him dry clothes to wear. He thanked her many times, and as he was walking away, she called out to him, 'Feel free to come here whenever you need a bath.'"

The granddaughter's thick laughter rolls out of her and she looks at the old woman who smiles deeply, as though she has heard the whole story.

"Good story," she says and squeezes the soft, moist hand that holds hers.

Shortly after this, after the morning's silence has returned to the bright room, the grandmother's eyes close and the girl lifts the frail hand from her own and places it just below her breasts. Then she leaves the old woman to sleep in peace, and prays that today will not be the day that life leaves her body.

SORAYA

30

....

CLOUDS

Summer L.A. and it is gray and sticky like how can you get out of bed when there isn't even school for distraction. Only chores and chores and TV and no more freedom than the mall and bad looks from everyone and nothing going anywhere.

With a grass-just-being-cut smell so loud I can't hear my thoughts but not loud enough to drown the ache. Springtime ache lasted too long this year and brought pictures of hillsides dotted with white and yellow and quiet, which I can just barely conjure up thanks to the damn lawn mower.

Who would think I would want to go back, just to watch my grandmother watching the day that sits slow and fat like a watermelon, watch the sky watching us, beg for the sun to cover us quietly.

My grandmother is dying and Ma is so sad. Everything here is so tense. Trouble thinking, trouble resting, and trouble making your bones relax and sink into pillows and routine. *Old age before youth is in full bloom,* says my mother's voice in the back of my mind. Worn out before anything has really started. *You are nothing without your virginity*. Lost in somewhere you grew up in, with a language you have taken, with a world that you want, but which is behind that clear steel curtain. *Watch it. Watch it all you want, but it will never be yours.*

My school counselor would say it was Uncle Haydar's fault. If she knew, she would talk about sexual abuse. But she doesn't know, and she'd be wrong anyhow. I choose what I do. I have always chosen what I do. We are in America now, so maybe Haydar could give me freedom, could get me to a life I can control.

Hala was given what she didn't ask for. Her bad luck is her good luck too, because it gave her freedom, gave her the chance to choose her own life.

One year away for me is a wedding, and then one little baby after another to change everything and cement it to impossibility. (No use complaining, they *will* be yours one day.)

Pain no one wants to know about hidden under the sink with all the dangerous cleaning fluids I must use just right, though I would rather wrap them up in a sandwich and eat them for lunch today. Fight not to accidentally give them to someone else, fight to tuck these feelings away out of sight.

I don't want a husband who walks under clouds, that is not my freedom. How can God mean this for anyone, a struggle that can never be won, a debt that can never be repaid. I sit silently and wait and pretend it does not exist, pretend there is no after-anything, that all there is, is now and I have to eat it up, devour what I can because there is no take-out service here.

Who would think I would want to go back, just to watch my grandmother watching the day that sits slow and fat like a watermelon, watch the sky watching us, beg for the sun to cover us quietly. And that will never happen now because she is dying and Ma can't leave the store.

No matter what, I won't let that noise make me forget. It will not be the one to steal my youth and spit my soul into the gutter.

Music loud, loud, loud, to drown it all and make my escape plan. . . .

31

....

LONG DISTANCE

Siddi (my father's father) has been staying with us for a while. He is very old and sometimes smells of going to the bathroom, but he tells us stories and pats our heads and sometimes gives us candies. He even says nice things to Baba for us, but it takes him some time to get the words out, and by then, my father loses his patience.

Once I heard my mother tell Monia that she thought Baba might be crazy because of all the things he did, but especially because he didn't respect his father properly.

That evening my father started talking about the sand that filled his dreams again. "How could you not be a little crazy when you have watched your dreams be buried the way I have?" he asked, as if he had heard my mother's conversation.

I miss my mother so much. Hamouda is crying a lot, even though Maysoun is over here all the time trying to help. The house feels vacant and Baba is too quiet, scary quiet. I want to call Sitti and tell her that I am sorry I never met her, but Baba won't let me stay on the phone, "And she wouldn't understand you anyway."

32

....

OLD MEN

A week and a half in Irbid and I feel I have slept a month and awoken with clear eyes. I have been back two days and am already twisting in Sharif's Fiat through Jerash for lunch. Selim's Restaurant. Fig trees hovering above. Dip your toes in the water as you eat. A place for lovers. A place for beauty.

I am very happy today. I love to drive in the car and put my hand out the window to catch the breezes. I know Sharif smiles at me in the rearview mirror when I do this, and I do not feel ashamed, though I do wonder what my father would think.

Sharif drops Latifa off at Jalal's (a minute away by car), but I do not feel like spending an afternoon with them, so I go home and find an empty house. Naguib Mahfouz comes with me to the tiny room off the kitchen. I am full with food and very sleepy. My book is very heavy. Silence is my blanket as I close my eyes and doze. So much to think about.

Then voices. My father thinks we are all gone. How long has he been home? There is another man with him and they are drinking beer, though it is still early in the afternoon. Voices and sounds and words I should not be hearing.

"Abu Mustafa," my father says, "I am a failure." I hear a click and I know I will soon smell his heavy cigarettes.

"Come now, Abu Jalal. You are being so dramatic and you have only had one beer. What is wrong?"

My father exhales heavily. "My wife is dead, may God have mercy on her. She was a good woman and no matter how many kind words I tell myself, I will always bear the burden of her death for not sending her abroad for treatment."

"Nonsense, Abu Jalal. It was God's will that her time on this earth of His had ended."

My father continues. "My failure is my son, Abu Mustafa. As you well know, my only son, Jalal, who from the day he was born has been the light of my eye, has just married a very distant relation on his mother's side. This girl who, granted, seems like a good girl and has the stamp of approval from Huda's sister, is a stranger to all of us. All his life he has been in Jordan. He only visited his mother's village three times. Yet his allegiance is to Nawara, to Palestine, not here. How can this be when his father is Jordanian and he has always lived here? It should not be like this. He did not ask me, he informed me. 'Father, I am going to marry a girl from Mama's village. Auntie Sahar has already found someone.' Can you imagine such a thing?"

"Times are changing, Abu Jalal."

I hear my father get up and then settle into the leather couch with a weary sigh. "My failures are also my daughters, Abu Mustafa, my dearest friend. My eldest daughter, Latifa, is decaying and causing those around her to decay with each breath she takes, while she spends her days smoking and reading her future in the bottom of a coffee cup. My middle daughter, Tihani, is in the Gulf, married to a reasonable man who has not divorced her even though it has been five years and she has not borne him a child. And my youngest daughter, Hala, is a stranger to me. She has learned to live in another culture and I no longer know what to do with her."

I feel my heart speed up when he says my name. Heavy words, decision words, are coming; I am sure of it.

"I saw Hala when she first came. She really is different from the rest! How does she like living with her uncle?"

"Very much, it seems, though she has not told me this. Two months she has been here and I really have no idea what to do with her, so I am going to put her on a plane back to the States. Hala is a kind girl and, you are right, very different from the others. She has her mother's spirit. I was prepared to marry her to someone—a relative—a very good man who would have been a good match for her, but imagine this: he refused me."

"What did he say was wrong with her?"

"That's what is so incredible. He refused me because he thinks she needs to choose her own life. 'If I have true love for her, which I must in order to marry her, I must allow her to be free. This is why I refuse you.' Imagine a man telling a father what to do with his own daughter." My father is silent as he drains the bottle of beer and sets it on the table. "And then I think, was I like this once too? So in love that I was willing to let go of the woman I adored in order that she be happy? It seems a century ago. And really, Abu Mustafa, I'm afraid that I was the opposite: I wanted her so much that I would sell everything to have her, but I did not love her enough to keep her alive."

"May God give you strength, Abu Jalal. Her death was God's will, and, as to the other, such is the way of our children today. You know as well as I that everyone is facing similar difficulties, though by no means am I trying to suggest that your problems are minor. It is almost as if there were a divide between the generations. Your children are all grown and you have done the best by them that you can, so now you must live your life as you wish and enjoy the last few years that God has given you on this earth of His."

A fat silence sits between the two men.

At some point the talking starts again, but relief has already sent me into a sweet and peaceful sleep.

I am not surprised when my father and I find ourselves alone together the next day, though this is something that has happened only a couple of times during my entire visit. Fortunately, we are in the car and provided with visual distractions to lighten the severity behind his words.

We are going outside the city to visit a cousin and pick up some sheep. Normally he would take Jalal, or one of the workers, but it is a short drive and only two sheep, so I go instead. We have not been driving in the shiny Toyota pickup —my father's "work" car—for five minutes when he says, with his eyes glued to the road in front of him, "I have been thinking."

"About what?" I ask with a twisty feeling in my stomach.

"I've been thinking about your situation."

My hands are clammy, though I am sure what his words will be.

"I think maybe you should wait to get married. I think you should go back to Hamdi and his Red, White, and Blue Wife and finish your schooling."

I have no words to offer.

"I am proud of you. It seems you are a very good girl."

"What made you decide all of this?" I ask him.

"You have changed since you've been gone. I can think of no one here who would be a good match for you now. Maybe in several years, or maybe not. Maybe you are better suited to marry someone who isn't Arab. I don't know. I think you should finish—or at least start—the university before you get married."

He is silent for a moment as the words sink into my skin. The gigantic relief I felt yesterday is even huger today. I feel I have been granted the greatest freedom.

But then the door slams back in my face.

"Did Sharif tell you he is going to be engaged soon?"

My heart skips a beat, but my father is oblivious and returns to his original subject. "I am sure it is best you go back. I will arrange your ticket for next week."

My father continues talking about Hamdi and how maybe it's not so bad in America, especially with so many cousins living there too, but I don't pay attention. All I can think of is Sharif about to enter into a marriage he has never even mentioned to me. I feel as though I will explode from anger at the thought, that I need to escape from the car.

One hundred years later we arrive at my father's cousin's house and go in for tea. I do not hear any words as we sit on the red rugs and look out onto the fields, though I am calmer, and more than anything surprised by my reaction to Sharif's impending engagement. After all, I am not in love with him.

The next day Sharif comes to take us to Ata Ali for ice cream, but for the first time Latifa declines the invitation. Any other day I would be ecstatic. Today I just feel empty and can't bring myself to say anything in the car. Even when we get there, I feel very far away as I listen to the pop music and watch the university kids chattering around us. I try to imagine myself among them.

"What's wrong?" Sharif asks me as the ice cream melts and dribbles down between my fingers.

"Nothing."

"What did you do yesterday?"

"I went with my father to pick up two sheep."

"Did you carry both of them?"

I don't laugh. "My father says you are getting married soon." I look in his eyes, but he doesn't look away like I expect he will.

"Listen, Hala. I am getting old. If I don't get married now, I never will."

"Who are you marrying?"

"I have an old friend who has a daughter. He says that I am the only one he trusts; that I am the only one who would do well by her. I told him I would think about it and I have."

"You're going to marry her then?"

"No. There is nothing wrong with her—she has a good sense of humor and is tall like you—it's just that I don't think it's fair to her. I think instead I may marry my cousin's niece. She is slightly cross-eyed, but very nice and pretty despite that."

My head is heavy, as though it may just plop down on the table in exhaustion. Thoughts getting closer; familiar comments making me giddy.

"Thank you for the ice cream," I tell him.

"Thank you for the company."

We walk out to the car without saying a word.

"What's the matter, Hala?"

I don't say anything. I feel my eyes burning and when I get in the car I stare out the window.

But instead of going home, Sharif drives through neighborhoods, then past them a little way up a hill to where there are no houses and you can see empty land in the distance. He stops the car.

"All this time, I thought you knew. I've been waiting for your return," he says after a moment or two of silence. "Your father insisted that you stay the summer because he wanted me to marry you, though now that you are here, I disagree with his decision."

I turn to him even though my face is burning, incredulous that I have been the subject of their conversations, that plans are being made and changed about my life and I had not the slightest inkling any of it was going on.

"If I were a selfish man, I would make you love me."

I feel my insides are being hollowed out. "Then you are a selfish man," I say in such a quiet voice I don't even know if he will hear me.

Because it is summer and afternoon, the seats are warm and the dry air is quiet around us, away from prying eyes and scandal seeking tongues.

"I cannot ask you to love me. I am an older man and I cannot give you what you need. I would always be good to you, I would always love you, but I am too old to expect that what I have to offer you is enough to keep you happy."

The sky above the brown hills is hazy and hot.

"That is silly," I say with my heart pounding everywhere. "So many marriages are between young girls and older men. Even you will marry someone who is just as young as me or even younger."

I can't believe I am talking about this as though it's the most normal thing, that I've spent the entire summer with a man who loves me and that I was oblivious.

"That's different. It's not just a question of age. I have explored the world and have come back to settle. You are seeing it for the first time. I think you have come back to say good-bye. Do you see yourself being happy here?"

I cannot see beyond today well enough to answer this question. I cannot see beyond the confused longing I have felt since the first day he came to visit.

We sit in silence for an eternity.

"We must go back now," he says. I need to say something in my defense, to make our togetherness last longer, but I cannot find any words. He turns to me and when I meet his gaze he pulls my face to his and our lips touch and cling for a moment, so gentle. I fold into his arms and feel relief as his body curls around me. Forever. Please be forever.

"I have a great deal of love for you," he says, and pulls away. He runs his hand down my flushed cheeks. "I want you very much. I want to make love to you and to spend every minute that remains in my life with you."

I want to stop this chain of events, to kiss his face, his eyes, his hands, but it is as though I've been struck dumb. I cannot find my words anywhere. He starts the car and we drive down, back through the haze and the peopled streets, none of the shouting in my head reaching my lips.

PART FOUR

33

....

NAKED UNDERNEATH

In the name of God, the benevolent, the merciful," I repeat until the plane is off the ground.

My father argued with me the whole time I was getting dressed to leave. (His decision to let me go back to America broke his dam of silence and we spent our final time together on very friendly terms.) "Why must you wear that? You know it is not appropriate. You are not going to a village or for a visit to someone. You are flying to America! Miss Modern Lady Who Had Almost No Interest In Dresses Until Today, why can't you wear your beloved jeans like you do all the time?"

It was endless, but no argument worked. I am wearing a *roza* that my grandmother made for my mother as part of her trousseau. My mother wore mostly western clothes—skirts and shirts or western dresses—but at home she liked *dishdashes* and this *roza*. I remember her wearing it and being happy. It is not a fancy one, but the pattern is clever and it suits me. I even imagine it still carries her scent. (I don't tell anyone that it is so hot that underneath it I am wearing only underwear—not a T-shirt and *shalwar* pants as my mother would wear.)

"You are a foolish girl," says Latifa. "Without the belt around it you look fat or pregnant and sloppy."

But my mother was several inches shorter than I am. If I wear the belt, the dress comes to the middle of my shin, which is impossibly short. I am not wearing the belt.

And so it went. Sharif came with a formal good-bye for me and a tiny envelope he stuck in my hand.

"Go off to your glittery America, rejoice in its prosperity, while our own country can be bought and sold," he said with a wink.

I didn't understand him until after he left and I opened the envelope: a gold charm of Palestine. I put it on my necklace. Now, on the plane, I run my fingers along the edges and wonder if he has already started making his wedding plans.

I am not at all nervous on this flight. There is no mystery and no worrying. No one is expecting a face I cannot offer. No, this flight is quiet. Two seats and no one to join me, to glare at me as I ache for Sharif. People do walk by and look at me strangely. Too young a girl with too short hair for that *roza* (a *thobe,* in their minds). I wonder if they think I am a foreigner.

I am starting over, starting over.

My mother is always with me. My father has not abandoned me, and Sharif has introduced my heart to something wonderful.

It is time to start something new, and something old, not to fix something unfinished. I will watch just the right way, to see the underside of things, the thinking things and the forgetting things, as my mother used to say. And then I will start university, and I will not come back in disgrace.

34

....

SAFE

A day like today is safe safe, like a mother's hand when it's not even considering slapping you even though you took some of her portion of the meat as well as your own. Gray enough you can't look naked, loud enough that no one can hear your stomach rumble because you didn't actually eat all that food but instead fed it to the stray dogs that hang around your house unless someone throws rocks at them.

Run your fingers against trees and bushes and grasses and fruits. They are like your neighbors, some prickly, some smooth, some little and hard, others soft and inviting.

"Everything has a corollary in nature," one of my teachers, Mr. Fayiz, always said. I can't see him running his fingers across tree trunks and through leaves, though one time I did see him run his fingers through Hiyam's hair.

But a day like today is also gray like old sadness that's been buried awhile, and gray like happy memories snatched by death returning to tempt you, to show you what is no longer yours, like my father.

Everything sharp like nails in your bicycle tire and beyond

repair and no money to buy a new one. Loud and crisp, every breath a statement, every thought a rumble.

The land is everywhere, too much in places, too lovely, too much yours and not yours at the same time. So you see why people like my father have heart attacks and drop dead on the street at the age of forty? Unavoidable. Stories are stitched under the skin at birth. Sometimes during a lifetime, or even half a lifetime, they can grow out of control and cause so much pain that you have to die to spare yourself the misery.

Days when sleep is your only goal, when a dreamless night would be a gift from God, when sadness is quiet happiness. Gloom when rain comes down like heavy mist and then like bullets and still you don't run to avoid it. Instead you walk more slowly.

Sometimes there are no stories, only feelings and still no words for those feelings, only pictures—that gray sky is my heart: vast and sick and empty. My own branches are breaking. Why every time when I open my eyes am I still here? That bird is my future, far away and uncertain.

Accept that which is God's will. Accept that which is God's will. Accept that which . . . I will accept.

35

....

FIRE

Scary is the day before Ma comes home and Baba drinks the whole bottle—I know because I saw it empty outside by his car—and he goes inside and Hamouda is figuring out how talking works and he looks at Baba and says "wild dog with a tick ass" plain as day like he's been saying those words since time began.

Baba sets on fire and I'm in the kitchen trying to be invisible and slap slap slap and the baby cries, so I go to see and Hamouda's arm is in my father's teeth and blood and then Siddi comes up to hold my father or to take the baby from him, and my father hits him hard, his own father, and knocks him to the floor and then goes back to the baby, who's just crying and crying and crying.

I do what I have never done. I run to the phone and dial 911 like they say to do in school.

"You are at 755 Marengo Street?" the voice asks.

"Yes."

"What's your emergency?"

"My grandfather is on the ground. My baby brother too."

"Did they fall?"

"My father is hitting everybody!"

I come back. Baba stops for a minute and stares and Hamouda stops crying for just a second and stares back, like he knows what my father could do. My father looks at his father lying on the floor, looks through me, and then he's down on the floor, right on top of Hamouda. At first Hamouda holds out his arm, thinking he's going to have hugs or get picked up, but then he feels the weight of my father's body and starts screaming even louder than before.

That's how the police find him when they come. My father's fire just goes away like it started raining inside him and he lets them take him, pull him off Hamouda, who I pick up from the ground as soon as the police pick up my father.

Scary is what is going to happen to us until Ma comes home. Scary is what Ma will do and if they'll say it's my fault.

I close my eyes tight and imagine she's here. "It's okay, little cucumber," I whisper in English in Hamouda's ear. "We'll be okay. We'll be okay, God willing."

36

....

JUST DOWN THE ROAD

I told Ma I was going to go with Hala back to Tucson because I wanted to visit Uncle Hamdi and Auntie Fay. I didn't ask her, I just told her: "Ma, I'm going for a week. I have the money. I'll help Hala buy her books and stuff."

No idea what made Ma let me go—probably figured how could I get in trouble in Tucson at the end of summer with boring Hala and boring Uncle Hamdi around; probably thought they'd be good influences. Hala's okay, actually. She just listens and doesn't make you feel like you're doing something wrong.

No idea in anyone's head that I came to see Uncle Haydar.

But Hamdi won't let me out of his sight. One day he takes me for a ride. Gets us Blizzards from Dairy Queen. Says, "It is a weakness of character, this need for a chemical shake mixed with candy, and stuffed thick into a cup."

Whatever.

Then he says, "You need to understand something." And drives us through their rinky-dink downtown, which takes all of one minute.

He drives down a wide street, then turns and pulls over. "I have to drop something off for Haydar," he says, already halfway out the door. "You can't come with me. You'll understand in a few minutes." He slams the door of his fly-looking, fully loaded Toyota Camry, engine running, air-conditioning blasting quietly, CD player grooving with some African drumbeat, and my heart in my mouth. No one said a word about Haydar. And how come it's all of a sudden and I can't go too?

Uncle Hamdi comes back before I can think of an answer and he gets in, but doesn't put the car in drive for a while. He just sits there, staring at the building he just stopped at and eating his Blizzard.

"Watch and you will understand. You need to understand, Soraya. I know what happened, what Haydar did to you. Just watch."

And so, for once, I do what I am told.

Watch him with his long hair and tamarind eyes as he leaves that downtown adobe house with bad plumbing and pissed-off cockroaches that fly, and walks down the street past the empty lot, past the falling-apart houses, the wild dogs behind chain-link fences, and the scorching day.

He doesn't mind leaving the girl asleep in his bedroom, isn't even thinking about her. Out. Out in the hot hot hot. He has to go out to be with the birds and the sky. To be away.

Watch him as he saunters down the street toward the park, as normal as anyone, as handsome as can be.

Watch. Watch and you will see what happens.

Fight like a tiger.

Watch him as he sits down at a picnic table in the shade, across from that bald man.

"I sleep with my eyes open," Haydar tells him and pulls

one of his brother's clean twenty-dollar bills out of his pocket without looking down.

The bald man does the same and they stare at each other with forty dollars waiting between them.

A crowd gathers. Anyone who is out wants the shade.

Eat the sky.

It doesn't matter how much time has passed; the bald man looks away. "Worse than a dog," he says to Haydar, who smiles and pockets the money.

Don't let the monkeys cover you with shit.

Watch him get up and walk away and then sit down on the curb next to a group of pigeons.

I saw you watching me from over there. Let me sit down and talk to you if you have the time.

He is oblivious of the two people in the car who are following him, watching him.

It's been a while. How have you been?

Words loud like lightning then so quiet they fall unheard on the sidewalk with straws and bottle tops and potato chip bags.

Shall we begin again and spend the afternoons painting again, or have you found another pastime?

He lies down on his back to watch the sky going somewhere from somewhere else. He lifts his feet in the air and giggles, not feeling the eyes plastered on him, not aware that anyone other than he is taking in this moment. After an impossible amount of time, he gets up, not pausing to let the blood leave his head slowly, and staggers for a moment before he walks away. His pace is quick, his skin healthy, his eyes focused, at least for the time being.

Where are you going? I need to talk to you. Please come back here.

There are whispers about him. Some stretch eight thou-

sand miles, others only go around the corner. There are rumors that something is not right—and indeed very wrong—
with this young man who used to be the fastest runner in
Nawara, his faraway, never completely forgotten, never entirely remembered village.

If you had asked his mother, she'd have said that it started
when he was a child and he saw his father killed. He went
blind for three weeks. When his eyes finally saw again he
stared deeper at everything and would go for hours without
blinking. His mother would say he did this in order to focus.
Everyone else said he did it because he had been touched by
the evil eye.

Dolls fill the night with unblinking eyes.

His eyes are large, languid, intense, often-unblinking-for-
hours. It gives people the impression that they are the center
of his universe.

Chase them.

He discovered that he could run very quickly. He won any
race with anyone of any age. He was the fastest runner in
Nawara.

Where have the mountains gone?

You can see that in him now as he walks down the sidewalk with purpose toward nowhere. His stride is long, his
body looks as though it will burst with stored-up energy.

He can be wonderful and he can be terrifying.

There was the time he came in second in a twenty-six-mile
marathon and couldn't speak English well enough to give an
interview.

There was the time he ran in the middle of the street to
pick up the little boy who had chased a ball and not seen the
car. He saved the boy's life and broke his own leg.

There was the time—in Los Angeles—when he went to his
sister's house for dinner during Ramadan and his nine-year-

old niece walked into the unlocked bathroom where he was jabbing a needle into his leathery skin. Her scream made him jump and his brother-in-law run and then shout and curse— if only he knew the whole story—and send him on his way, which turned out to be back where he started.

No one knows what goes on inside. It's been a while. Most of his friends are elsewhere, and most of his other friends are women. You might be surprised at the number of young women who have seen his beautiful eyes as they stare into their own and who have been flattered by his direct gaze. They enjoy his intensity, enjoy what they believe to be attention and devotion pouring from his eyes. They can tell he has lived a large and tragic life, which is why they accept his erratic behavior as moodiness, his ability to sleep for twenty-four hours as general fatigue, and his midnight walks and talking to birds as a love for nature.

Asleep in his apartment right now is a going-in-the-right-direction girl. Nineteen years old. As American as apple pie and arcades and health clubs and Supporting Our Troops and teenagers having sex. She was blinded by his unblinking eyes, wooed by his foreign tongue.

I see deserts back there.

It started like that for her, like a rock slide, like a dream.

How it progressed for him is something else. More like a bicycle in molasses.

He sleeps with a knife in his hand. Even when he is not alone. Scared the shit out of him waking up and seeing blood all over that girl's face. At first he did not realize what had happened, that the knife was so razor sharp she did not feel a thing when she put her hand around it and squeezed. He washed the blood off and bandaged her hand.

"Why do you sleep with that?"

"Have to be armed. Thieves flood downtown at night."

"Why don't you have a gun?" she asked as the last of the blood swirls down the drain.

"Might have to use it."

He wishes she would leave. He doesn't like that she is always there. Thinks for her own good she should leave.

Upside down isn't good unless you can see the sky.

"What?"

He leaves instead. Goes to the park. Lying on his back in the grass he watches the clouds as thick as herds of unshorn sheep roll thickly across the painfully blue sky. He wears the sun's heat like a blanket, does not shade his eyes to avoid the glare, which appears from behind those continents of cotton. They are so close he begins to wonder if God is approaching him, if He is about to offer him a blanket other than the sun's heat. He stretches his hands up to grab the thick white rolls and is surprised at how far away they are, how unattainable.

Come lie with me. Cover me.

We are driving away now after driving around. Following my own uncle, and all I want to do is scream or puke, but Hamdi keeps talking, back to his Economics Professor voice, so much louder than the voices in my head.

"So now you know. Your uncle is like other men you see, except this one lies on his back in the middle of a city park and talks to pigeons and imitates statues. Clinically speaking he is bipolar, paranoid schizophrenic, but for real life he is crazy. For home he is crazy. Not one hundred percent crazy, but walking toward it at a rapid pace, catalyzed by God knows what monster inside him. We try to help, but there is not much we can do—there is not much anyone can do. I think you needed to see him now, while you can still recognize him."

Uncle Hamdi is quiet, letting his words sink in.

I sit, staring at nothing, maybe at yesterday. I want to puke or punch something, but Hamdi's voice won't let me.

"The fall will come. It hasn't yet, but it will. It's just down the road."

We move slowly along the streets in our bubble, but then Hamdi pulls over under a tree, puts the car in park, and stares in front of him. "Soraya, I know what Haydar did. I know it has caused you a considerable amount of grief. I am willing to help you in whatever way I can, whether financial or otherwise."

How can he know? Like Haydar long ago, I am dumbstruck. I came here looking for an escape, and I am being handed one, and I don't know how to use it.

"Soraya, I want to do what is right, to help you find what is right. I have told no one, and I will respect your wishes, as you are a young woman, not a child. You can always come to me, but please, for your own good, forget about Haydar and who he was. That person is gone. It is so hard to accept, but he is gone, whether because of his illness, or because of the drugs he takes, he is gone. Please, please don't think of him as an alternative."

Hamdi's English words sit between us on the leather seats, like uninvited guests that squeeze you and make you want to scream. I can't even cry. I want to get out of the car, but I can't move, can't speak.

Hamdi stares for a bit, then starts driving. I don't know where we are going, but I need to move and I am thankful that somewhere in his controlled little self, he understands that. He doesn't even mind when I turn up the music, loud, and close my eyes, lean back in the seat, and go as far away from here as I can.

HALA

37
....

BARE WALLS

*H*amdi and Fay have a nice house in the center of the city that suits them and their professor lifestyle. I have my own private room in the back that looks out on an enclosed patio. Bougainvillea climbs up the white walls and makes my view pink- and salmon-colored. Inside, however, the white walls are bare because that is classier than having photos and posters scattered all over the place.

The house is decorated in high-class American style, no knickknacks, no faded pictures, and no Muhammad mosaics. Neat encyclopedia, nineteen matching volumes. High-class halogen bulbs. Chairs that make you cross your legs. Lush carpeting, even in the bathroom. No cold feet or need for clap clap clap slippers to wear in the house. The temperature is regulated between seventy-three and seventy-eight degrees, even though we are in Arizona and it is very expensive to do this. High-class American blah, no soul, no colors, only outside walls that wandered in and stayed. Show-off house with no heart or fancy bracelets.

Funny how this never bothered me before, how I almost didn't notice it.

Maybe Hamdi is trying to fit in, have a house sturdy and plain like everyone's moods. Maybe they both like this look. Maybe they see it best not to imagine as you gaze at the walls, that it's best to sit in silence.

Everywhere I look is clean, neat, Navajo white. There are no photos and only one painting in the living room. It is a grayish, whitish abstract. I cannot imagine anything when I look at it. I might as well just stare at the wall.

In my house in Amman, which I always think of as "my mother's house," because it was so much in her style, every nook and cranny filled with something: a plant, a book, a statue, a flower, and every wall was covered with religious plaques, calendars, photographs. Every gift and every souvenir ever received or bought was on display like a trophy. Always somewhere to look to take you somewhere else, to make you think. Either a memory resurrected or a new place to go or a joy to feel. Only way you could not think in our house would be if you closed your eyes and imagined nothing, which is impossible. No spare wall space. No place for thoughts to stop.

Nothing like this fancy, scrubbed-clean, no-imagination house that makes me deadly tired like a full day just past and I haven't gotten out of bed yet.

Four days back. Maybe it is not so exciting because it seems very permanent. This is now my home.

Hamdi took Soraya on an errand. (I am sure it is to Dairy Queen. He is supposed to be on a diet, but I have caught him sneaking Blizzards twice already.) Fay is at the University. I am alone with the white walls that never bothered me before, and longing, so much longing for a home that doesn't exist anymore, and I close my eyes again and go back, just like that, eight thousand miles in the blink of an eye. Hamdi would not approve. He is the opposite of my mother and does not believe in staying late in bed unless you are dying.

"How do you expect to make it in this country if you don't work harder than everyone else?" he says.

What I want to know is how you expect to make it in this country if you're wandering around with a knot the size of yesterday in your stomach.

We see it all differently. He needs a routine and starkness to make it, and I need clutter and memories. How could I have lived here for three years and not been bothered by this? Maybe because it was never mine before.

Curled up under a cool sheet, hugging my memories and drifting, I imagine everything, from going through customs to smelling the dusty afternoons; from eating fresh garbanzo beans to playing with Ma; from hiding from Latifa and then, zoom, to Sharif, where I linger, linger, linger. Like yesterday and like tomorrow and then by accident my eyes pop open and what slaps me in the face?

Empty walls.

Slam them shut again with picnics and visits, with trips to the *souq,* with trips to the country, with hours of cooking and smells so rich they make you queasy, especially if it's Ramadan and you haven't eaten all day but still have to cook a feast for after sundown.

I dive headfirst into this box of photos and stay inside until they paper the insides of my eyes. Soon it won't matter what our walls are like because every time I look up I see Ma smiling at me, or Sitti peeling carrots, or Latifa spilling the tea on a prospective husband.

Remember for yourself and for your tomorrow, my mother used to say. Remember to make your day new and old, but be sure to think of something you never thought of before. If you don't, your life will be like having your foot stuck in a mouse hole, looks small and harmless, but holds on tight and won't let you go until something comes along to change the landscape.

Eyes squeeze close until they hurt, longing for the slopes of the land around my father's house, longing for my mother's sweet voice to fill my ears with the stories of her village: her poor mother, stuck with all those kids; Haydar, now crazy, who—*now you have to promise not to tell a soul*—saw the men who did it and probably was the one who killed them; the hopelessly dumb and forever multiplying Sulayman family—one of whom is now part of our family; and, best of all, wise old Abu Salwan, who carries his Bedouin wisdom in his eyes and has gold hidden away in the desert.

Remember the stories of Nawara: everything, including the tragedies. Remember this one, whose house was built on American money and now stands empty as he waits for retirement age, hoping he will not have a heart attack before then, hoping the Israelis will not move in before he comes home. Remember the ones who left, who fled, whose memories are vague and lives are changed. Remember the young men in their prime, who work twelve-hour days, driving taxis, running grocery stores, selling merchandise door to door. Remember all those women lost in different ways, with no tomorrows. Remember the young ones, who came here as babies, but who cannot remember what they have not seen and therefore have no reason to behave.

Eyes open slowly, the white walls are softer.

I get out of bed and go to the box where I keep all my pictures. As I go through them one by one, I put a few aside: this one overlooking the farm goes over my desk. This one of me with my mother goes on the dresser. This one of Latifa dancing in her loud, blue dress at my brother's wedding, this one will go next to my mother on the dresser. And this one that Latifa took of me with Sharif, this goes by the bed.

The day goes on. I take the extra car and drive to the mall to buy frames of all sizes and colors. I pass a travel agent and ask for posters of Jordan. They only have Morocco and

Egypt, which will do. By evening the bare walls are bearable, lively, different and familiar. I sit on the floor and stare, then close my eyes. It is deep nighttime in Amman—and in Nawara—and I have tucked my memories under a scratchy blanket, wishing them the sweetest dreams as I open my eyes to a new, but not unfamiliar world.

ACKNOWLEDGMENTS

My gratitude to the Fulbright Foundation.

To the Abu Saud Sawaid family, Marwan Mahmoud, Houri Berberian, Jimmie Harris III, Pam Grammer, and Helene Atwan, great thanks for all of your time, patience, and generosity.

To my mother, Margaret Halaby, thank you for your encouragement, love, and incredible attention to detail.

To my husband, Raik, and my children: *alf shukr wa shukr* for your endless support, patience, and love.